OBLIVION

A MEDICINE MAN NOVEL

Written By
JOSHUA RYAN OGG

HEATHEN

ONE

ALMOST THERE, JUST A little more.

That's what he kept telling himself with every scrape and scratch. His fingers were bleeding and sore as they ground a shrinking piece of orange chalk into raw exposed brick.

As Above, So Below.

As Above, So Below.

As Above—

The symbol took shape on the wall, an image held in his mind a hundred times and in dreams a thousand more. He dug his fingers into the symbol and the gritty clay behind it, scratching aggressively into the wall with chalk and blood and pain.

He could make it go away, he knew it. Those tugging, distracting, nagging thoughts and memories. With enough focus he could drive out the guilt and banish the haunting voice in the back of his head that reminded him that he, Kalvin Renley, was some kind of monster. Some twisted thing with poisoned thoughts and too much power.

He tried to concentrate, to adjust his thinking. This was part of the process. This was the ritual.

As Above, So Be—

Steam came shrieking out of a boiling kettle across the room and brought Kal out of his trance. He stepped back from the wall of symbols and art to see the large twisted spiral and the various witchy glyphs he had been scrawling across his workspace.

"Look!" shouted a shrill, gurgling voice from across the room. "It's almost done."

Acrid green smoke filled the messy shack and Kal rushed to the steaming kettle to adjust the heat and toss in a final pinch of sulfuric phosphate. Just the right temperature, just the right mix.

The gelatinous liquid that flowed through his massive, winding chemistry apparatus held Kal's only hope that his gifts were good for something pure. His fingers ached and he had grown light-headed from the smoke. The mad chemist continued to mutter prayers over the concoction, tapping his mind into something greater than himself. That was the only way to keep his demons out of the brew. It was the only way to make medicine out of the strange, twisted magic that flowed from Kal's own soul.

For the final ingredient, a drop of his own blood, straight from his index finger, still caked in chalk and red brick dust. It was this last part that made the brew something more than just chemicals. It was the trance and the bargain, the sigil on the wall, and the state of mind.

It was the blood, sweat, pain, and madness of the man that made the stuff *medicine.*

"Keeping your shit together?" asked the alien voice, still hidden in the shadows.

Kal studied the green tonic and the symbols on the wall. He'd known only nightmares for weeks and a gut instinct that something dark was on the horizon.

"Hardly."

TWO

THE NIGHT HAD become a drizzle, wet and chilly, and the dark-haired twenty-something stumbling down the sidewalk alone was shivering beneath her oversized jacket. Her bare feet were blistered and sore but they kept plodding along the wet pavement in a part of downtown she'd never seen before, carrying her away from an unforgettable stint in some personal version of hell.

A car drove by, startling her from her own troubled thoughts, and she crouched defensively against a closed storefront. The visions were relentless. No matter how hard she tried to block them out, focus elsewhere, or just plain outrun them, Eden's mind was plagued with horrifying thoughts and persistent nightmares. It wasn't just the masked faces out there pursuing her, there was something else. Something that followed just over her shoulder, always watching, always breathing itchy torment down her neck.

The night itself may have been watching her, for all she knew. Everything was amplified and neon, the drugs still lingering in her bloodstream. She'd been awake for days and on the run for hours.

Colors screamed at her and the stray thoughts of others seemed to find their way inside her head.

Eden tried not to look up when people passed her on the sidewalk. She ran her hands through her thick dark hair, feeling shame like a sickness in her stomach. Fingers trembling, lip quivering, Eden couldn't remember the last few days too well at all. She'd been careless and lost her head. Should never have been there.

What's wrong with her?

A couple watched her as they passed. Judged her. She could hear their voices in her head.

Look at her...   ...Tramp...

Hooker? Poor kid's on ...meth or crack or something.

Whatever they do now...

...Disgusting...

They weren't alone. Others were nearby, people active in the late evening hours of downtown, and they all had surface thoughts that reached out to Eden.

Fuck is rain doing in SD?

Stupid puddle, these shoes are new...

...Dirty bastard, I'll kill him for that.

"Almost there, Edie," she cooed to herself in a calm but quivering voice. "Just keep going."

The place wasn't hard to spot once she turned down the alley off of Sixth Avenue. The girls at the bus stop had told her this would be the spot to find him. Hole-in-the-wall dive with a few rowdies hanging around the entrance. A small wooden sign over the door read *District 7*. Eden took a deep breath and gathered her courage.

Please be here, she thought.

Eden slipped between two drunks near the door and stepped inside. District 7 was a squat little watering hole with a handful of rough-neck regulars nursing tumblers of dark whiskey.

Oof whadda we have here?   *....Hey girl...*

Damn, what a piece....

Her head was still swimming with lysergic colors and stray thoughts but she made her way to the bar. Eden had gotten used to the slimy thoughts that raced through most peoples' minds but tonight, in this place, it was just a bit more difficult to block them out.

"I'm looking for Donnie DeGrassi," she said to the stone-faced man with stringy grey hair behind the bar.

Of course you are...

He grinned at her and nodded toward a booth in the back.

Eden saw a wild-haired Brazilian man seated in the booth texting on his phone. She swallowed hard and made her way across the bar.

"Are you, uhm— Are you Donnie?" she stuttered awkwardly and the man looked up.

"Who's asking?"

...what's this, another one of Donnie's playthings...

—just what we need right now...

"I'm looking for the medicine man," Eden said, hoping to skip the awkward parts.

No shit, babe. Who ain't?

Goddamnit maybe he's got something to do with—

The man sat up straight and looked around to make sure no one else was listening.

"You're barkin' up the wrong tree, kid," said the Brazilian. "Nobody's seen the witch doctor in months."

"And Donnie?"

He stared at her a moment.

"Donnie's not here," he said. "Leave your number and I'll have him get in touch."

Eden felt herself grow desperate and afraid. She tried to listen in on the guy's mind but his thoughts were erratic and uncontrolled. He was afraid of something and distracted by a man called Goldie and an obsession with some black powder. She felt the breath on her neck, the eyes watching...

"You don't understand, I... I need to see the medicine—"

"Look, beat it already!"

The Brazilian had enough on his mind, he didn't have time for this.

...bigger shit to deal with.... Fuckin' tweekers and tripsters....

E D E N . . .

Eden's heartbeat sped up as she heard it...

E E D E N N . . .

It called her name in a slick, slimy guttural whisper that crept up her spine and gripped her neck. Eden froze and began to shiver in fear. The Brazilian man was staring at her, almost hostile now. The room was getting foggy and the colors blinded her. Sound was distorted and amplified, just like her heartbeat, and she felt dizzy.

"Stop..." she started to say but it only got louder and the voice of that *thing* was so close.

Whoa, what's her deal, is she—

"PLEASE STOP!!" she screamed over the music and chatter.

Those nearby paused to stare at her, that crazy girl standing there sweating and dizzy. Her panic had her heart thumping and blood was starting to seep from her ears. The Brazilian looked at her in horror like she were some kind of freak.

She couldn't stay any longer. Eden stumbled dizzily out of District 7 and onto the cold, wet sidewalk.

She saw it in someone's mind. A small shack with a man inside.

That man could help her, she was sure of it.

Wherever he was.

All she could do now was curl up in a ball against the cold brick wall in the alley and try to block out the thoughts of others, the visions of torture, and the creeping sensation of the curse.

THREE

A SLEEK BLACK JAGUAR F-TYPE cut hard across three lanes of Interstate 8 and took the exit for Downtown.

"I said I'm on my way, Miles, chill the fuck out."

Donnie DeGrassi wore a black jacket against red leather interior and his Italian leather shoe worked the gas pedal like he was competing in the Indy 500. He gripped the wheel casually with one hand, his iPhone pressed to his ear with the other, as he whipped across streets and allies in the Gaslamp district of downtown San Diego. Sharp green eyes dove in and out of the rear-view mirror as street lights flickered across the windshield.

"I'm pullin' up now. Order me a burger."

Donnie ended the call and pocketed his phone.

Miles, he thought as he shook his head. *They don't come any more high-strung than that.*

The Jaguar careened through an alley and roared to a stop outside of District 7. Donnie killed the engine and took a moment to pinch the bridge of his nose. Had the spins again. So much shit on his mind these days, it was all he could do to stay lucid. Pulled a couple more blue star caps from a pill bottle in his pocket and popped them in his mouth to even things out.

"Here we go," he said to himself and stepped out of the car.

He paid little attention to the drunks by the door or the tweeker girl slumped over on the sidewalk. They all noticed him though. Everyone noticed Donnie DeGrassi. Chiseled Italian features, slick hair, and a steady gaze, he was a man of the streets with connections and allies in every slum and high rise. Everyone's friendly neighborhood ambassador of high-flying substances and roller coaster trips.

"Donnie!"

It was warm inside the bar and that distinct orange glow of cheap light bulbs brought life to the grime on the walls. Donnie gave a couple handshakes and fist bumps to familiar faces as he made his way to the bar. Fella working back there was a stringy-haired corpse of a man that went by the name Sampson.

"How's business, Sam?"

Donnie reached across the bar to put a brotherly hand on Sampson's shoulder as they smiled in greeting at one another.

"Bout as good as it can these days," Sampson grumbled.

Donnie nodded. Noticed Miles waiting for him at the table in the back. "This guy order me that burger?"

"Should be ready in a few minutes," Sampson answered. "To go?"

"You betcha."

Donnie continued on to the back booth where his buddy sat waiting. Miles was a wild-haired Brazilian that never looked bathed or rested. He'd been knocking back shots of Patron while he waited for Donnie to show. Already had the shakes and shifty eyes.

"You look like shit, Miles."

Miles looked up and the relief that washed over him was obvious. He moved aside to make room for Donnie to sit.

"Thank God, DeGrassi, fuck!"

Donnie sat and kept an eye on the rest of the bar. "What's got you buggin'?"

Miles knocked back his last shot and ran his hands through his hair.

"It's Goldie, man," said Miles. "I haven't heard from him since this morning and he missed a drop tonight. No call, no show."

"Idiot's probably passed out somewhere."

"No, Donnie. I don't think that's it."

Miles had always been a basket case but Donnie couldn't remember the last time he saw the guy this worked up. "You think it's this new shit he's been runnin'?"

"I told him that dust didn't sound legit, man. Called me freakin' out real early this morning. Said he wanted out, something went wrong. Someone got sick from it or something, I don't know but... Goldie was... I ain't never heard him scared like that, Donnie!"

Miles paused and fumbled with his empty shot glass, fingers trembling.

"Who's the clan?"

"Not one of ours," Miles said and looked up to meet Donnie's eye. "El Brujan."

Donnie looked away and tried not to scoff. He didn't put much stock in ghost stories and everything he'd ever heard about this mysterious new Mexican cartel just reeked of bullshit. Drugs were hot in Southern California, everyone looking for wild rides and exit portals to new worlds. There were a few decent chemists out there putting out designer compounds and the clans that sprung up to traffic them were nothing if not eccentric. Donnie was a skeptic but he was also a businessman and couldn't afford to discount the possibility that el Brujan were real and possibly slinging bad drugs.

"This the black dust I keep hearing about?"

Miles nodded. "Oblivion. I hear it's bad news, man. Real bad news."

"How could you let him get involved with the Brujan, Miles?"

"I tried to talk him out of it, Donnie! Don't put this on me, man, don'! I can't handle—"

"Alright, just chill," Donnie said to calm him down.

"Something don't feel right, Donnie."

"Keep your feelings to yourself," Donnie said. "Just lay low for the night. We'll put the word out and track down Goldie in the morning. You hear anything else about these Brujan cats, you hit me up, got it?"

Miles nodded but was quickly distracted by the girl that had suddenly appeared at their table. She stood there awkwardly, staring down at Donnie with those big haunted eyes. He shifted uncomfortably under her gaze.

"Uhm... can I help you?" he asked, not really meaning it.

Eden's hair was a wild mess, her makeup a smeared swamp, and her pupils shook as erratically as her fingers.

"I need to see the medicine man," she said.

Donnie gave Miles an irritated glance before responding.

"Sorry, he doesn't brew anymore. And get your shit from a runner, I don't deal direct."

She stared at him in motionless silence, haunting him to his core.

"Please," she whispered, dangling on the edge of desperation.

Donnie took a breath. True addiction and helplessness is a sad thing to see. One of the reasons he liked to keep his distance and work through mirrors and runners.

"Look, I want to help you, kid. I do. But the Medicine Man's been...retired. For a while."

Sampson brought Donnie's burger to the table and sat it down in a brown paper bag. One glance at the awkward girl and he asked, "Everything okay, Donnie?"

Donnie nodded and Sampson returned to the bar. Eden continued to stare at him as though she were looking right through him, sifting around in his soul for the answers she sought. Donnie stood and grabbed the paper bag.

"Get yourself cleaned up," he said to her. "Miles, relax until we hear something real, alright?"

With that he made his way to the door. Eden followed him, zeroing in on his distant thought patterns as he jumped in the shiny Jaguar and sped off into the night. She stood there in the chilly evening air, watching the color trail disappear with the car, lip quivering. For Eden, the Jag left a wake of ephemeral color along the alley. Just enough for her to follow through the night.

Miles appeared on the sidewalk behind her. "Maybe I can get you what you need," he said.

She shook her head. "I doubt that very much."

FOUR

THE BLACK JAG PARKED at the end of Del Mar Avenue, a road that dipped steeply off the hill and hit its dead end at a rocky outcropping south of the Ocean Beach pier. Donnie stepped out, adjusted his jacket, and gave the block a once over.

Quiet night, waves crashing, streets empty. Donnie moved along the sidewalk at a contained hustle. He wasn't the hurried type. His clothes were tailored, his hair trimmed neat, even had an approachable friendly face but his default expression said he could cut his way through bullshit.

He strolled up the sidewalk trying not to think about Goldie and the cartel rumors. In fact, he was more haunted by that girl at the bar. It didn't used to be that way. The stuff Kal used to make turned junkies and lost addicts into inspired artists and activists. It was a genuine miracle but those days came crashing down and now here they were. He was still keeping the game going but without the real medicine. It could only go on like this for so long.

The action wasn't in O.B tonight, at least as far as street clans or drug rings go. Donnie wasn't here on business anyway. This was more of a personal favor for one of his oldest associates, which required a visit to his oldest friend.

That old friend was actually the more complicated part. Donnie was comfortable with the loose alliances of underground megalomaniacs and the exchange of illicit substances but there was another side to things. It was a strange side he didn't quite understand and one he was perfectly happy to let his old buddy handle.

And so here he was.

Following a footpath that wound through an alley behind a shop called *The Black* to a split in the rocks, Donnie made his way to a place very few had ever been. Tattered tapestries and torn clothing hung on lines between the crumbling walls and alien symbols were etched into the sandstone. The path continued up the slope to a small beach shack that overlooked the water.

If you didn't know it was there, you likely never saw it. That was the point. Its inhabitant didn't want to be found. He used to be easy to find, developed quite a reputation for bizarre voodoo-inspired concoctions, but these days he kept to himself. He'd become more of a legend than anything real, the whole county wondering when *or if* his creations would come back on the market.

They called him the Medicine Man.

Donnie couldn't remember who said it first but it was a great code name so he ran with it. He used it to create a brand that channeled his friend's inspired substances to eager minds all up and down the coast.

Kal was a genuine mystery, eccentric and radical, the kind of hookup everyone wished they had. A twitchy star-gazer that brewed the most advanced psychedelic compounds on the coast. Soul chemist, tripster shaman, alchemical artist, and pure bat shit fucking crazy. AKA The Medicine Man.

Place gave Donnie the creeps.

It was usually close to midnight when folks around the neighborhood reported strange sounds or lights in the sky. Animal noises and guttural chanting, usually. Sometimes punk rock played too loud. Paired with the bizarre smells that came from the secluded shack, it wasn't hard to keep people to minding their own business. It was through a broken window where a beach towel of black crows billowed in the salty breeze that the repetitive thrumming of a guitar amplifier blared across Ocean Beach and the air reeked of sulfur and burnt hair.

Donnie buttoned his shirt sleeve and braced himself. Entering Kal's world was a head trip not for the faint of heart.

INSIDE THE BEACH SHACK there was smoke, there were lights, and there was reverb.

THURMMM   THURMMM   THURMMM THURMMM

The electric cadence reverberated around the tiny shack and filled the haze of smoke with multi-colored lights and a distorted drone.

"This is the gateway. The Omega door."

THURMM THURMM THURMM

"Zoso lives in the eternal sea."

THURMM THURMM

"Think I'm getting somewhere," said the bundle of messy dreads and almond skin slumped over on the thirty watt amp. Kal was concentrating, strumming the vibrations to build his trance, eyes squinted studiously through the haze of bong smoke and incense at the wall of madness before him.

The wall was a mess of crumbling drywall and cracked faux-wood paneling with a library of occult symbols, graphs, and equations layered across the surface in overlapping patterns. Stars and pentagrams and the sigils of archangels, planetary alignments with zodiac charts, alchemical formulas and quantum equations. There were charts and doodles tacked up, graphs and print-outs and finger painted maps, strange patterns and formulas scrawled with shaky hand in chalk, ink, paint, dirt, and blood. A mad man's cave paintings.

"You're getting nowhere," said a raspy voice from just over Kal's shoulder.

"Shush," said Kal. "There's a pattern..."

THURMM THURMM THURMM

He'd been staring stoned at his wall of symbols and equations for hours, strumming his Les Paul in the hopes of deepening the trance to plumb forth more precious inspiration and insight.

No dice.

"You're just giving yourself a headache."

"Quiet," Kal murmured.

The source of the second voice moved forward into the light, perched on a chair next to Kal. The shape resembled a small animal, a shadow in the smoke with eyes that glowed an ember red. As the creature crouched into the light, however, it revealed something much less common than a house pet. With a leathery-skinned body sprouting wings and a tail, the impish creature came straight out of some twisted nightmare in Kal's head, smoldering with an aura of smoke and looking around with giant swirling, hypnotic eyes.

"You're not helping," Kal grumbled.

The imp picked absently at his toe talons and grumbled, "You been at this for hours. The spirits all agree; the D chord is shit for inspiration."

THURMM . . .

Kal sat the guitar aside. "I hate when you're right."

His little psychedelic spirit pet was better than a voice *inside* his head and kept him entertained.

"Donnie's here," said Meklyn, followed by a timely knock at the door.

Of course there was also the psychic advantage of a spirit pet.

"Great."

Kal rubbed his eyes and shook off the stupor of the last few hours. He surveyed the massive chemistry setup in the kitchen, a writhing mess of tubes and beakers pumping some radiant liquid through a network of distillation. The color looked right, steam hissing out the release valve. Batch was almost done.

"Second!" he called.

Swatting Meklyn aside, Kal crossed to the door. He paused to slide his finger down the door jamb across several little runes etched into the wood. Each one popped and smoked as his finger passed over it. Protection wards. A guy brewing semi-hallucinogenic occult pigments in a homemade still with his invisible pet from the underworld has to take precautions, right?

He popped the door open and gave his friend a nod.

"Smells like ass," Donnie muttered.

"Missed you too," Kal replied.

Donnie stepped inside and shut the door. He didn't make it far, stopping in the middle of the room to take a sweep of the scene.

Place was a dump, a scattered mix of unwashed clothes, empty energy drink cans, half empty bottles of Jim Beam, a righteous water bong on the coffee table, and a microwave that looked like it tried to heat a missile. The shelves were cluttered with an odd assortment of voodoo dolls, hash pipes, vintage vinyls, animal skulls with squiggly little symbols etched into the surface, pop comic books by the stack, tribal masks, and piles of old vellum books. On a desk cluttered with sea shells in the corner glowed the screen of a laptop that boasted a flickering multi-colored Jimmy Page as its screensaver. Above it hung a surf board painted in skulls and feathers. Burn marks and blood stains littered the carpet and there was no sitting on that ratty tweed couch responsible for the piss mildew smell.

"Jesus, man," was all he could say. "You alright?"

"Yeah, why." It wasn't a question. Kal wasn't even paying attention.

Kal shuffled around in pajama pants and a Dead Kennedys T-Shirt. Long ratty mess of dark jungle hair, his skin a mixed toffee hue from some who-knows American shake-up. Five o'clock shadow.

Tattoos across his muscles that twisted down his right arm to a big glaring Eye of Horus on his palm.

He was the absent minded professor to Donnie's slick salesman, the kind of guy who does yoga and surfs when he's not summoning spirits and tripping balls. The kind of lost soul that stands in the middle of the room and stares at his wall of mangled symbols and forgets to breathe.

"Kal, this place is a dump," said Donnie.

Kal twitched. "This is my sanctum, Donnie. A little respect."

"You gotta get out, man."

"I'm busy," said Kal, staring at the wall.

Donnie looked it over and saw only nonsense. Picked out the giant spiral painted in orange over the whole thing.

"Fuck you tryna solve here anyway?"

"Coming alignment of Jupiter with Leo crosses the thirteenth sun spot cycle since Solstice and McKenna's Timewave Zero is a trending hashtag under a new moon. Adjunct is twelve degrees and I keep going back to this tilt to the Pleiades during winter sol—"

"Forget I asked," Donnie muttered. "The hell you do to yourself?"

He grabbed Kal's hand and took a look at the bloody fingertips. Kal looked at him but was clearly a million miles away, staring at him across the Universe through dilated pupils.

"Here," Donnie said, shoving the brown paper sack into Kal's arms. "Eat something. Come back to Earth."

Donnie turned and made a beeline for the chemistry set across the room. Made it a point to cross in front of Kal to break his focus on that hypnotic board of star crap. Kal sat and tore into the packaging around the burger. Picked off the meat and slowly ate some of the vegetables.

"That the stuff?"

Kal nodded absently as he choked down the ketchup-slimed lettuce and gagged, vomiting it back up in the corner.

Donnie ignored him and edged closer to have a look at the brew. Kal's work space was a violent clash of science and voodoo in a slob hippie's beach shack but his products never missed the mark. The island bar off the kitchen was crammed with an elaborate tangle of plastic tubing, beakers, and copper pots that looked like a cross between a chemistry set and a homemade still.

Wiping his mouth, Kal stumbled into the kitchen to rustle through an assortment of junk. Donnie couldn't tell what was trash and what was actually part of the process. It was all piled together. Kal twisted a knob on the copper pot that released a bout of steam into the air. He readied a small glass vial and waited at the spout as a green liquid plumbed its way through the tubes to drip out into the bottle.

"Gonna take a day or two for full effect and she has to drink the whole thing," Kal instructed. This was his artwork he was handing over and he never took his eyes off it. "Got a bit of a dizzy kick to it and the comedown will be harsh."

"Long as it does the trick."

Donnie marveled for a moment at the potion his buddy had cooked up. The edge of weird and sophisticated. Only a handful of chemists on the coast could brew the kind of high quality substance people wanted and only Kal brewed the real magic.

"Thank you."

Kal shrugged, found a half-eaten granola bar on the counter, and crammed it in his mouth.

"Some weird shit happening out there, Kal," Donnie said as he slid a pile of books off the only chair and plopped down.

"Yeah. Eleventh blue moon since 9/11..." Kal rambled through the mouthful of granola.

"Ain't like the old days," Donnie continued. "Gangs are all riled up, some new drug on the street no one's ever heard of, making people go nuts. Some messed up shit. I haven't seen the stuff. East Side Locos got involved. Who knows, man, the Game is so—"

"Donnie," Kal interrupted, finishing his work with a stopper placed on the glass vial of green syrup. "I'm out, remember?"

Kal handed Donnie the vial. Sweet strange medicine. The only work he did anymore.

"Right," said Donnie, pocketing the elixir.

There was a time when the mention of some new compound on the street would have gotten his buddy's attention and the duo would go tearing up the highway to check it out. But times had changed. Kal was still in a dark place, soul searching or whatever, but Donnie knew how it worked. No one's ever *really* out of the Game. Least of all the Medicine Man.

"People still asking about you," Donnie said in the silence. "Lookin' for help."

Kal was silent a while, staring at the orange spiral on the wall. "Something's coming, Donnie. Dark visions and... Something's coming. Something bad."

Donnie couldn't help but think of what Miles had said earlier. And that tripped out girl.

"Why don't you run this with me?" he urged. "Do you some good to get out, man. See your meds in action. See people."

"People," Kal echoed. "That's your wheelhouse, Donnie. I'm good. ...on my own."

Donnie knew to pick his battles.

"Suit yourself," he muttered.

Donnie crossed to the door and they both let the silence linger another minute.

"Don't be a stranger," Donnie said and ducked out into the evening drizzle.

Kal followed him to the door and ran his finger up the strip of symbols to reactivate the wards with that familiar static charge. He could feel the *snap crackle pop* in the air as the energy resumed its effects. Gave a nod of appreciation for the subtle sciences and collapsed exhausted onto the couch.

Meklyn appeared in a flash of sparks and smoke. "Another quiet night in, Doc?"

"Piss off," Kal muttered and tumbled into sleep.

DONNIE WALKED BACK to his car with a heavy weight on his chest. Something about what Kal said rang true. It did feel like something big was coming. Or maybe it was just the contact buzz. He dipped into the Jag and peeled off into the night.

FIVE

THE CANVAS BAG SCRATCHED his face and it smelled like dung. Goldie didn't know how long he'd been tied up in the back seat of the black Hummer but they had to be out past the Alpine Desert by now. The ride was bumpy and the men packed into the vehicle around him offered a swift elbow to the nose any time he spoke. Blood from his broken nose had dried to his mouth and chin, molding the bag to his face and all he could think about was the torture that lay ahead.

Goldie felt the vehicle slow to a stop and muffled voices spoke in a language he didn't recognize. He knew he was in it deep. He'd been stupid, let his guard down. You don't pull that crap in this game. That's how you lose.

Now the ride had come to an end. Goldie Two-Shot of the East Side Locos may as well have been a helpless child as four hands gripped and jerked him from the seat. They tore him out of the vehicle and tossed him across the desert sand. He stumbled, rolled, collapsed, hands still tied behind his back. The sounds of at least four booted soldiers moved around him and two of them dragged him thirty feet across the cold desert sand to drop him in a heap beneath the stars where he lay still and aching for what seemed an eternity.

Poor Goldie had been beaten to a pulp, bagged, gagged, and hauled off to the California desert without his aggressors saying so much as a word. When they spoke to each other it was a cryptic foreign tongue he'd never heard before. To think, just yesterday he was in a little massage parlor in La Jolla getting a happy ending from one of Queen Carly's girls. Now the hood was being ripped off his head like a stuck bandage taking a piece of his face with it. Bat shit terrified, he grunted back the pain and let his eyes adjust to the surroundings.

Took a minute for the world to swim into focus, all blurry at first and stinging from the sweat. His captors numbered more than twenty, fanned out in uniform black combat gear, their faces hidden behind bone skull masks. Each stood at attention with an assault rifle poised at his chest, motionless specters against the night.

El Brujan.

Goldie had never seen them all assembled. The only contact he had as their point man for the San Diego market was a boney man in a dark suit who always wore red lensed sunglasses, even at night which was the only time they ever met. This was more than a new clan, this was a death squad posing as a cartel. His hands shook and his lip quivered. The clans were telling stories about El Brujan. People called them demons. Their drugs were curses, their violent threats not idle, and they answered to a man they called *el Diablo*.

"P-Please," Goldie stuttered, his pathetic whisper a squeak in the still night. "People are getting sick, they—Gah, they're dying, man! Please! I had to. I had to! You gotta understand…"

The soldiers stared like lifeless wraiths.

28

Goldie's shoulders slumped.   There was no reasoning with them, this was something beyond all that. He had betrayed them and if they were even a shadow of the big cartels, he was double fucked. He sat there in the creepy silence and waited, suppressing the tremble of his lower lip.

A foul chill crept up his spine as one of them finally stepped forward.   The masked soldier's heavy boots fell slow and deliberate across the parched sand. He crouched down low and leaned toward Goldie, feral animal eyes looking out through that skull mask.

"You stink of fear," growled the voice behind a boney face.

Goldie's lip quivered. "Look, man, I don't want—"

The soldier punched him hard in the nose. Blood splattered across the white ground and Goldie fell silent.

"You've done enough talking already," the man said in a low, gravelly voice. "Do you know what we do with traitors?"

A sinister wind blew cold past Goldie's sweat-drenched face as the soldier touched his leering mask and slowly pulled it off. The skull slipped down over a sharp nose and the sight of the monster made Goldie, a grown man, tremble and wet himself right there on his knees. He lowered his head, tried to look away, but some magnetism forced him to look at the beast.

The man, if you could call him that, was hairless and scarred. Every inch of his head and neck was tattooed in intricate tribal designs that laced together with precise scars and lacerations.   Stitches remained in fresh cuts and what flesh wasn't touched by ink or scar was scorched and calloused from repeated flaying. It was a grotesque and disturbing mutilation etched across the face of a square-jawed animal.

The man who had ordered this done to himself eyed his prey with feral eyes that burned somewhere far away. His pearl white teeth were filed to sharp fangs and Goldie swore he caught the flick of a forked tongue.

"You fail to answer," he spat. "Do you know what we do with traitors?"

Goldie shook his head. Wanted to speak. But just shook.

The monster called el Diablo stood and paced around Goldie Two-Shot like a panther stalking the night.

"First our answer to thieves," he said.

Goldie shook as the man dropped to a knee behind him, a vicious hot breath on the back of his neck.

"You stole from us before you betrayed us, didn't you?"

"No, p-pleaseuuAAHHHH!"

Goldie's begging melted at the swift cut of the devil's blade.

He screamed as blood gushed from his hand, a stump still bound behind his back. Those heavy boots stalked calmly back to the front and Goldie's nightmare crouched down low again.

"Ahh, God! Ahh, you... Y-you cut..."

"When you cross over to meet your gods," the monster hissed, eyes like burning points of light. "I want you to tell them that Xechan sent you. Their time is over. The war has evolved."

Goldie stared in horror as the hideous Xechan casually bit down into one of Goldie's two severed digits. Blood ran down his chin as he slowly ate his prisoner's fingers. Swallowed. Stood.

Goldie leaned forward and cried into the sand as the shooting pain and shock took over.

Xechan waved a soldier forward and the man brought a bulging burlap sack which he dumped at Goldie's feet, toppling a collection of freshly-severed human heads out into a pile of slimy gore. Goldie Two-Shot stared in horror at the faces of his fellow East Side Locos, his friends and brothers on the crazy streets of the Millennium. His clan.

"UUAANNGH!" Goldie wailed and then vomited into the dirt along with a few more "Aghs!" and "Uncks!"

Leaving Goldie doubled over in sickness and defeat in the stench of human gore, Xechan turned slowly and walked to the edge of the circle.

In his place, two soldiers stepped forward with ornamental red chalices. Goldie looked up at the sight, two black pillars on either side holding up ritual cups.

"Por favor el Diablo, *I beg you—*"

"Begging is for dogs," growled Xechan with a nod to his men.

While their prisoner continued to scream and plead, the Brujan soldier-priests poured the contents of the cups onto Goldie's head, soaking him in the acrid odor and sharp sting of gasoline.

His mind raced, his heart kicked into a panic. He was going to burn.

"No, please!" Goldie begged pathetically.

This was the end, he knew it. He dreaded it. Saw the flames in his mind, felt the searing pain deep down in his guts. The raw terror of the agony that would send him into darkness took hold of his muscles, his voice, his thoughts. He screamed and babbled, grasping at life.

"Please, I beg you! Please!..." he screamed and babbled. "God, please! Mother!" and finally "ANGH! NO!"

Xechan looked up at the stars, aligned perfectly with the planets, and drew a deep breath.

"A new sun rises," he said in prayer to the night. "Let it be born in blood and fire."

A match appeared in his gloved hand. He struck it. Flicked it. And to the sounds of Goldie's screams, the match went tumbling end over end through the air to land in the poor bastard's lap.

Flames engulfed the soldiers' sacrifice in a cocoon of exploding pain that ripped the flesh from the poor man's bones. Goldie Two-Shot's screams rose shrill and terrified into the night. The soldiers of El Brujan, clad in ritual black and skeletal masks—the legion of *el muerte*—fanned out around the man who burned alive in their midst. Xechan stood in the center with his sacrifice and his men brought the five severed heads to the five corners. The fire worked its way across a design of gasoline in the sand, forming a large angular star in the night.

El Brujan burned their message into the naked Earth and stood proud.

The bound hostage and the heads of their enemies aflame at Xechan's feet, he looked to the stars and smiled.

So it begins.

SIX

KAL WAS DREAMING. He knew it by the sound.

His board cut a cresting silver wave and the water parted like butter. Surfing the water, up and down, feet gliding over the waves, orange California sun swollen to bursting in the sky.

And then there's Heather.

Sitting there on the beach with those cute hippie-girl dreads and that knitted scarf she made herself. Eyes as bright as a newborn, looking to Kal like he's the very sun itself. Scenes flit by like a fast forward through his memories, a trail of breadcrumbs to the ending he knows is inevitable, that point when the film reel breaks and there's just the clicking of the shutter.

Another wave breaks.

That roller coaster at Six Flags, up over the top... inch by inch...

She trusted him. He promised her the world.

He cut across a steep swell and caught the tube just as it formed.

She took the tab, a little yellow compound he put together.

Told her they would ride ecstasy over the edge or some romantic bullshit in the moment.

He felt the water spraying over his face.

It was a metaphor, of course, going over the edge. Kal would never be that reckless. Would he? It was only supposed to be a trip. A glowing experience and then a return. Together.

The waves crashed and the board tumbled from beneath him. Kal fell beneath the waves to the blue-brown washing machine below. He had miscalculated. Something went wrong. She trusted him with those big doe eyes and Kal had failed.

It was right overhead like a black hole in the sky. A man burning to death in the desert. Skeletal faces and black masses. Something dark was on the horizon...

He had failed. Wasn't ready.

Fallen under the crashing waves.

"WAKE UP!"

Kal resurfaced to consciousness, greeted by a knocking at his door and Meklyn's swirling red orbs just inches from his face. He shoved the creature away and sat up, rubbing the dream from his eyes.

"Damnit, Donnie."

"Not Donnie," Meklyn gurgled and crawled up the back of the couch.

Kal stood and shuffled to the door to peer through the keyhole. It was dark but that figure sure wasn't Donnie's.

"Nobody home," Kal called and held his breath to await the sound of trailing footsteps.

"Please, I'm sorry, you don't—" her voice choked. "I have this..."

A long pause.

Kal listened into the ringing silence as this stranger's sniffles turned to cries and her cries to sobbing, some defeated girl leaning her life against the sawed timber that separated his insane little world from... *Out There.*

Kal stared at his disheveled reflection in the mirror across the room.

Stupid girl, asking the genie to come out of the bottle...

"You're my last hope," she whispered.

Don't be stupid, Kal.

The moment lingered like that piss mildew smell, Kal debating with himself, until he finally sighed and opened the door just a crack.

"Who are you?"

In the tiny fissure between the door and the jagged frame, his eye leapt around like a searchlight scanning the outside world.

"Oh um..." she quickly wiped her tears aside. "I'm Eden. I'm—"

The pale orange of the boardwalk lights silhouetted her shape like a goddess and the door jamb groaned in warning.

"Mother of Kali..." he swore, the words born on their own like some spontaneous prayer.

Eden shivered beneath the long coat that hugged her slim frame and dark locks of hair fell over her face in frazzled clumps. Poor thing's pupils shook erratically in place as her lower lip quivered sick. Dark visions flashed and flickered in her mind, Kal could see them, and somehow this little shack gave her hope.

"I don't brew anymore," he said. "Get your fix somewhere else."

"I don't want a fix," she said, desperate to keep the door open. "I want fixed. They tell me you can fix me. They say... you're the medicine man."

"Is that what they say?"

She gave the wild-haired medicine man a pleading look and whispered, "Please."

Kal just wanted to go back to sleep, maybe slip into the oblivion of his subconscious and be alone. But the fates were restless. Then he spotted it. Right there in front of him, dangling from a thin black cord around her neck. The orange spiral. An omen...

"Damnit," he grumbled.

Kal surveyed the trash-strewn footpath stretching out beyond his comfort zone with a wary eye. The lurking things that haunted him were out there, shadows and astral footsteps the only signs of their unrelenting hunt. A sick feeling did somersaults in his gut. Some omen was teasing him, something he didn't understand. Something was about to happen.

"Get in here."

He shuddered with a chill, pulled the strange girl through the drafty portal, and slammed the door closed behind them. As Eden crossed the threshold, the wards on the door jamb fizzled, smoked, and popped with loud cracks telling Kal some bad juju was in the house. He took a step away, eyeing her suspiciously.

"Who are you?" he asked again.

"My name is Eden and I'm... sick."

That was the best the poor girl could come up with to describe her *condition*. The tormenting thoughts and psychic visions, a walking nightmare with a demon lurking in her gut. They don't write prescriptions for this sort of thing at the clinic.

"What do you want?" He scanned her aura best he could but it was clouded and dark. All Kal could see was a dangerous puzzle.

She looked only at her feet and held a long pause before whispering, "There's something wrong with me. Something bad."

"*Junkie*," Meklyn gurgled from his perch atop the bookcase.

"More than drugs," Kal muttered.

"Please," she begged. "I don't have anywhere else to go."

He tried to shut her pleas out of his mind. He was done with this responsibility. This reputation. This penance. What did this poor creature think he was capable of? What miracles was she hoping he could conjure up to wash away her sins?   Kal preferred the solitude, just him and his own brand of crazy.

"Look," he started. "This isn't my jive anymore and I don't really think I can—"

Eden couldn't help it. An involuntary shriek escaped her lips like a banshee's wail and froze Kal mid-sentence. Her hands instinctively cupped her mouth but the bomb had already been dropped.

"Sorry," she said meekly.

Kal stared unblinking in the ensuing silence.

Meklyn didn't hesitate to prod the awkward moment, "Found one crazier than you."

"What?" she asked.

Eden was sure it was the embarrassment and her own confused thoughts but she swore she heard another voice in the room.

Bat shit crazy, that is.

Enough, Mek.

Wh-h-Her deal? Cursed, addicted, l0st... se7enth circle and the red planet's ring—erpp...

Eden stared at Kal as his stray thoughts and telepathic conversation with Meklyn bled through into her perception and the hair on her neck stood on end.

...half the people in OB probably heard—is that a dark spot in her aura—cancer of the soul, bad juju and the wards // half time out here // Meklyn put up a seal...

"Stop…" she whispered faintly, averting her eyes and trying to draw focus from the floor.

Lesser Banishing of the Penta—earthairfirewaterspirit…

>   *What'd she say?*   *Can she…?*

>   *Wait…*   *Is she reading my…?*

>   *….///….///….*

And suddenly there was silence in her head. Just her own thoughts again. Her own fear.

Kal Renley and a girl called Eden, the medicine man and a cursed psychic addict from the streets, they stood in the dissipating smoke, the clean and open air of the mind, and stared at one another.

Oh.

Oh?

You can hear me.

Yes?

Yes.

What is this?

Safe.

No doubt she was more trouble than she was worth but, for that one moment, Kal didn't feel quite the freak. Enough of her memories were dancing in the corner of his perception for him to understand that something significant had brought Eden to his doorstep, bad timing or no.

"What happened to you?" he asked in a low, cautious voice.

Eden looked away in shame.

"Is it the visions? The voices?" he asked.

"Please," she trembled. "I don't know. The visions I could always handle but this... this is new."

Kal tried to relax and shake off the persistent stray thoughts escaping her aura. She had seen truly dark magic and brought the scars of it with her. He looked to his wall of bizarre cyphers and noticed only the spiral ringing it all in together.

"Tell me everything," he said.

Eden shifted uncomfortably.

"It's, erm... Well, it's hard to explain. Do... Do you have some water?"

It took a moment for the request to register. "Oh, water, yes."

Kal scrambled nervously through the kitchen for a clean cup and some water.

Something's not right with this...

"Quiet, Meklyn," Kal said, shaking off the distraction and returning to the girl.

"What?"

"Nothing. Here," he said, holding out the water.

She took it gratefully and sipped. Before long she was gulping, getting it down as quick as possible. Eden wasn't sure when she last stopped to eat or drink.

"Thank you," she said.

"Now, tell me everything."

She hesitated a moment, lip quivering with nerves and sickness. "It's better if I show you."

She turned slowly and lowered her coat to reveal several inches of porcelain flesh. Kal watched anxiously, muscles tense, as the fabric slipped down below the ink on her back and—

BAM!

Hit him like a shovel to the face.

A hundred intricate black slashes formed a sigil tattoo from shoulder to shoulder, the kind that raises off the surface to greet you, a living patch of ink that clawed its way inside Kal's head and raised its quills.

"Aghfuk!" he bellowed, staggering back several steps.

A mind trained for symbol recognition and perceiving deeper meanings suddenly recoiled defensively as the nasty mark blasted right through his wards and defenses on the spot, just one glimpse. Nasty jagged bastard of lines and dots and—

"Stop!" Kal heard himself saying as he tried not to melt down from the knee-jerk panic that ripped through his body like a primal instinct. Pure fear writhed its way through his intestines and when he looked away from the image, that symbol, that tattooed blasphemy on her back, it was already burned into his mind.

"Curse! Shield your mind!"

Meklyn's warning faded into the white noise as incoherent syllables tumbled across Kal's lips in response to the sigil's enervating negative energy. The curse drained him of his life force right there on the spot, vision swimming and the world spinning.

Eden leaped to her feet and backed tearfully toward the door.

"No no no, please, this can't be happening," she pleaded. Her demons had followed her here and even the witch doctor seemed unable to help.

"Mek…" Kal gasped as his knees gave out and he toppled to the floor in violent spasms, an astral plague ripping through his body.

"ElO bAn Ahriman…" he heard himself gurgling into the carpet from far away, his body wracked with pains and violent surges as the demons took hold through the open door.

Meklyn's voice broke through his thoughts, *"Banish, you bastard, banish that thing!"*

"…Can't!"

How could this happen?

Kal hated himself for letting it surprise him. He was the fucking medicine man! He protected his mind from symbolic invasion on a daily basis, worked with dark conjure for a goddamn living, and this bitch's tattoo sucker punches him right in the third eye?

Mek, I can't get it out…

He felt it nesting already in the slimy folds of his subconscious and somehow he'd failed at his own game. A snake expert taken out by venom.

Eden was horrified. She burst into tears and kept repeating "Oh god, I'm sorry, I'm so sorry..." as she backed away to the door.

Kal tried to raise a hand to stop her but he was shaky and weak.

"You have to shut it out," Meklyn hissed. He was protective of Kal's mind—that's where he lived, after all—but this one had gotten the jump on them both.

"I'm sorry," Eden stammered in horror and guilt before disappearing into the rain-soaked night.

"No wait," Kal pleaded but the curse was sending him into shock. The effects of that sigil still writhed inside his head and, for a moment, he wasn't sure if he was really this cosmic millennial medicine man that had spoken to gods, wrestled angels, and banished demons or if he was just a delusional addict with severe psychological issues.

Probably both.

Images of horror and shame raced through him and he thrashed violently. Something was on him, chasing him down the long halls of his mind. Something that got inside him with just a glance at that symbol.

Heather's death, the clan violence, the shadow hunters on the astral plane, all the things that drove him into seclusion and out of the game, it all swarmed his mind at once. The cabinet he had been holding shut for months came bursting open to spill the slimy contents of his repressed subconscious into plain view.

He stumbled toward the kitchen and crashed through drawers and shelves in search of something to ward off the effects. He was looking for something specific. His own special tonic. His *Joos.*

But he knew better. He didn't keep any in the house. Had a slight problem staying away from it when a supply was on hand. His own little vice. But now he needed it. Whatever curse had been embedded in that girl's ink was currently kicking the shit out of him from the inside.

Kal managed to get to his feet, the world spinning and screaming around him, and stumbled out into the rain. Only one place in this neighborhood kept the Joos.

Kal stumbled, sick and puking, through the night, wavering on the edge of a mad abyss, looking and groping for help, for a fix of his own. For his own medicine.

SEVEN

It was late, almost midnight, and Donnie kept his head down and hands visible in a neighborhood like this. South Imperial Beach wasn't far from the border and cozied up against the naval ship yards. Turf belonged to a gang called the Gear Heads. A close-knit mob of hulking giants, the Gear Heads ran a sizeable smuggling operation out of an old ship hangar near the docks at the bottom of Coronado. Mostly cocaine from down south, the occasional group of refugees, standard stuff.

Tonight they were expecting Donnie as a friend and courier but their neighborhood was deserted. The only signs of life for blocks were the pigeons huddled in flocks down the alleys. Donnie kept his eyes peeled. There was a certain way to approach protected clan turf and, like most organizations, each clan had its own quirks and protocols.

Here, in the Gear Heads' neighborhood, it was a matter of walking toward the warehouse defenselessly until they found and approached you. Not Donnie's favorite way of attracting the attention of hardened killers, but he and the Gear Heads went way back. Didn't take them long to show.

The welcome committee was just two guys but their combined shadows blanketed the sidewalk as they rounded the corner from the warehouse. They had to weigh three bills a piece, both over seven foot tall. Donnie recognized them immediately. Ratchet and Diggs were two of the biggest bastards alive. Not that well-proportioned gym look either. They slammed sledge hammers and welded steel ships all day so their arms were a couple of giant oak trees, all corded and bulging like a sack of cannon balls wrapped in skin and soaked in motor oil. Hard motherfuckers.

Donnie stopped in front of them, about chest-high, and looked up.

"Fellas."

Ratchet nodded for him to follow and turned to lead the way. Diggs offered the same stoic nod and fell in line behind Donnie. They marched silently through streets of long shadows and jagged brick walls. Everyone had their theatrics, that's how the streets worked. A big Game, that's what they all called it. A dangerous, serious, decadent Game.

At the end of the lane they came to a massive warehouse that loomed over the neighborhood like an old abandoned fortress covered in soot. The sound of clanging metal and grinding steel could be heard even at this hour.

Ratchet swung the door open and stepped aside.

"Boss'll be glad to see you," he grumbled.

Donnie figured as much.

They passed into the Gear Head Fortress and the volume cranked up on the sounds of welding and grinding. Some power rock ballad wheezed out of an antique cassette stereo. The boys were working on something big in the far hangar bay, a tank maybe, the orange sparks lighting up that side of the building like fireworks.

But it wasn't that side of the building that had business for—

"Donnie DeGrassi," rumbled a familiar voice. "My old friend."

The figure that waited for him in the shadows to the right towered over him like Goliath. Donnie stepped closer and let his eyes adjust.

The leader of the Gear Heads was a mean, gruff old sonovabitch, name of Darby. Shoulders that could carry a steam ship and hands that could juggle bowling balls. Almost seventy years on him, hair greying and thinning, and still he had the reputation of a gruff old goat who liked to break a man's arms for offending him and much worse for crossing him in a bad deal.

But this wasn't the man Donnie once knew, and that's what haunted him the most.

"Darby," he said.

In a word, Darby had withered. Guy hadn't bathed in a week and slouched instead of puffing out that Buick-sized chest. His eyes had a sad, faraway look to them, something sad in there. Darby came straight over and, to Donnie's surprise, wrapped him in a big bear hug that lasted a long, awkward moment. DeGrassi didn't know what to say. Grief does strange things to men. He gave the guy a warm pat on the back.

"I thank you for this, from my heart," Darby said, looking Donnie right in the eyes with that haunted, troubled look.

"Don't mention it," said Donnie, groping in his pocket for the green vial and holding it up to gleam in the light. "In the name of friendship."

Darby looked on the thing with a kind of sacred reverence and awe.

"This... will work?"

DeGrassi reached up to put a hand on the brute's shoulder. "I have absolute faith in the Medicine Man."

Wasn't a lie necessarily. That hippie was in one of his sulking drugged-out hermit binges but Donnie had faith in Kal's drugs, even if Kal himself didn't.

Darby nodded. "As do I. Shame Kalvin couldn't be here."

"He's, uh, yeah. He's a busy man," Donnie dodged.

"Let's not waste more time," said the Boss and suddenly they were walking out the back.

Darby led Donnie, Ratchet, and Diggs through the warehouse, out the back door, and across a large junkyard to a dusty little yellow house surrounded by a picket fence. The boss liked his place right next to the shop. Kept it cozy, even in a minefield of junk debris. Like a little doll house, the bungalow seemed laughably tiny for a guy the size of Darby.

The porch creaked under their combined weight and the screen door rattled as it opened. The guards waited at the door as Darby motioned Donnie into the house. They stepped into a cozy little living room with photos on the wall and flowers on the coffee table. Place was given an added dimension of cramped as the enormous host ducked through the low door and took up half the room.

Several of his equally overgrown family members were asleep on couches and bedrolls across the floor. Food trays sat out along with cards and sympathy gifts. Donnie got goose bumps, noting the strange cross between a funeral vigil and the waiting room of the ER. And how did this many enormous people fit comfortably into such a small little house, anyway?

Donnie felt awkward entering the private residence of the Big Beluga himself. Kept his footsteps quiet as he trailed Darby down the hall, past the kitchen, to a little bedroom door near the rear of the house.

Darby creaked the door open slowly. The room was painted in bright colors and adorned in princess décor. A Hello Kitty night light banished the darkness and there, in a little four poster bed, snuggled beneath massive hand-made quilts, was a girl just now seven years old. Darby's daughter, Mia.

"Darby, are you sure I should--?"

"Come on," was all the big fella mumbled as he dropped to a knee at the girl's bedside.

Donnie wasn't sure what to do or say. The sight of her there, looking withered and sick and starving, it tugged on his heartstrings more than he liked. The wall over her bed boasted an Irish Cross and across the room was an assortment of Celtic knot symbols, hand woven from vines and roots.

"Quack doctors all but gave up. Gave her a few weeks," Darby said as he fished the vial out of his pocket and popped the stopper. The smell of peppermint and some strange lacquer filled the room. Haunted whispers crept out of the shadowy corners. "Time to put our faith elsewhere."

Donnie had absolute faith in Kal, something he could say of no one else. He'd seen the guy pull off a few completely unexplainable stunts, miracles some folks called them. Donnie saw him brew up compounds that shouldn't be possible, things that melted the boundaries of the world. But this was a helpless child. Darby's child. If something went wrong...

Darby tipped the elixir gently to Mia's lips and it trickled into her mouth. She coughed and sputtered, some of it dribbling down her chin. She struggled with it, still half asleep, and almost choked, her skin flushing with a sickly green. For a second, Donnie was worried. Darby didn't seem bothered as he gently wiped the dribble from her chin.

It started slowly. Mia's veins bulged green through her pale skin and she began to shift around uncomfortably. She gasped at a loss for breath, her hands shaking. Darby looked up with concern but all Donnie could do was nod for reassurance.

They waited and watched as Mia fought the strange medicine, tension like a bubble in the room.

She mumbled gurgled nonsense from the trance of deep sleep, "Ag0ra fin de @ndro saXon, yln jesTliC m3xi qu@nta fiR!" her body contorting and writhing in the sheets.

"Donnie..." came Darby's concerned whisper but Donnie didn't dare move.

Don't let me down, buddy...

Somewhere across town Kal was thrashing around in fits. Donnie couldn't really see it but it was there, in his head. It happened sometimes. Kal was thrashing around on the sidewalk like a monster going through fits and coughing up black tar.

Mia shifted and twisted, sweat beading on her face and running down her cheek.

"Papa..."

Darby nearly leaped to take her hand at the mention of his true name and she smiled.

Kal... somewhere out there in torment, and Donnie just watched. Waited.

Come on...

Then, just as suddenly as it began, the struggle faded. Mia stopped, let out her breath, and relaxed softly into the bed. Color flushed back to her cheeks and she sighed comfortably. Her breathing resumed, her veins disappeared, and she slept. Peacefully, she slept.

Relief washed over Donnie like warm bathwater.

Darby knelt there for a long time, in grateful prayer. Raw emotion etched into his face as moisture seeped from his eyes and traced the lines down his cheeks.

"Kal said it would take a day or so to work through her system," Donnie explained quietly in the ensuing silence.

The big beluga stood and placed one of his massive paws on Donnie's shoulder.

"Tell our friend Kal that I am in his debt."

Donnie nodded. "Let me know how she does."

Darby pulled him in for another crushing bear hug and Donnie thought of Kal going through some hellish transformation or sickness or something. He hoped it was just a bad piece of his imagination. With Kal and this weird hoodoo, you could never tell.

A few minutes later they were walking back across the grass and gravel to the warehouse. The sounds of clanging work echoed through the drafty open air and Darby's burden seemed to have lifted from his shoulders just enough to breathe. He stood taller and less hunched over in fear and grief. Hope does wonders for folks, that was the secret of this business and it kept Donnie DeGrassi in the Game. Darby offered him a rolled cigarette and they stepped through the side door into the shadows of his workshop.

That's when Donnie's phone went off. Darby's followed.

It was probably business but Donnie's nerves were shot and he wanted a couple draws on the smoke before diving back into deals. Darby on the other hand checked his phone and Donnie could tell by the big guy's sickened expression that the news wasn't good.

"Sweet Christ, you gotta be kiddin' me," Darby grumbled. He looked away.

"What is it?" Donnie asked.

"Don't know the number. You get it too?"

Something felt incredibly wrong as Donnie reached for his iPhone. Checked the message. It was a picture from an unknown number, all sixes. When he opened it and looked, it took him a minute to register what he was seeing.

Five bloody severed heads on pikes and a body burning in the center.

The message read: SO IT BEGINS

"What the fuck..." was all Donnie could muster.

"That's the East Side Locos," Darby said. "Whole crew."

Donnie nodded, not sure what to say. He put his phone away. If Darby got it too, the picture had to have gone out to everyone. At least all the clan heads.

"You heard of this uppity spic calls himself el Diablo?" Darby grumbled, drawing on his smoke.

Donnie accepted the light and gave a nod. "The Diablo of El Brujan. Can't go a fuckin' block without hearing about 'em now. New rival to the Mexican cartels."

"Looks like cartel work to me," Darby added.

"Year ago nobody ever heard of 'em. Next thing you know they own half the turf in Mexico and they're making plays at the border."

"Just drugs?"

"Fuck, who knows. Just got on the scene but, shit, they got no problem loppin' off heads," Donnie said. His hand was shaking as he pulled on the cigarette.

Donnie watched the Gear Heads weld together not just ship fittings across the warehouse but an army tank in the back of the shop. These guys don't fuck around. "Heard they sling some new shit but I don't know what it is."

"That's what bothers me," Darby grumbled. "Guys in Santee call it Oblivion, this new shit. It's bad. Not just cause it's knocking kids right on their asses, puttin' tweekers into comas. But it's carving into the local market, Donnie, cause once they try this shit they're either hooked and want nothin' else... or they're out completely."

That last part hung in the air. Donnie kept thinking of all the things Miles had said earlier. About Goldie freaking out about something he wanted out of.

Darby pulled a long drag on his smoke, the fiery tip burning bright in the shadows of his warehouse. "Can't have some two bit beaner poisoning the whole marketplace, Donnie."

Donnie watched the guys welding together their tank in the wee hours of the morning, his mind clinking through the gears. Troublesome thoughts to consider. Something was brewing on the streets and it could turn real bad real fast. It was already going to be a mess.

And Kal says he's out of the game.

We'll see, buddy. We'll see.

EIGHT

THIS WAS HIS TRANCE.

The deep belly growl of the Jaguar as it flicked through gears was like Donnie's war cadence as he raced her up the 101. Dipping in and out of traffic and smoking doors in long stretches, there was only one way to truly outrun your problems. The salty air tasted sweeter whipping by at a 120 mph. Murders and lies and criminal trade seemed a thousand miles away. Out here on the edge of the Western world, beneath palm trees and stars, it was like riding the knife's edge.

Donnie couldn't think of any other way to concentrate. Kept hearing Miles' words in his head.

"Told you it was fucking Brujan, Donnie! Oh my god, we're dead..."

Thinking of Kal was even worse. The shack in OB was the first place Donnie went once he saw the pentagram in the murder photo. Thought Kal would have some insight, or at least take interest. But the shack had been ransacked and Kal was gone.

"Damnit, where are you buddy?"

Everything's unraveling, DeGrassi, he told himself. *Clean it up.*

He couldn't shake the image of carnage either. The heads of every member of the East Side Locos all stuck on pikes like some bloody medieval throwback. There hadn't been a real death in this game in almost two years and never a clan wipe. This was big. This would kill the Pax for good.

Quick reaction to tail lights and Donnie's slamming on the breaks, shifting gears, and whipping a wide arc on the shoulder to weave around a car turning across lanes. Gassed it back up to sixty five and kept the wind flowing through the windows.

This was his zen.

The truce between the gangs was something he worked hard for, much to his own benefit. He and Kal, that is. Despite his buddy's early exit from the scene, everything was going great until someone was dumb enough to kill seven hustlers and poison the market with a dangerous new compound. Fucked it all up. Everyone afraid to buy, not sure who to trust. It would all be a mess now.

His phone was blowing up in the passenger seat but he had ignored it. Too much to piece together. Donnie had gotten used to the way things were. It would get riskier now that blood was on the ground. The game had leveled up. He climbed on the brakes as he approached a red light.

Another ding. The iPhone sat on a silver briefcase he picked up in Coronado half an hour ago. He grabbed the device and made his obligatory message check.

ATHEN   you pick it up yet?

AMY	hey =)
MILES	close?
BIANCA	how you been?
CHASE BANK	Text back Yes to confirm funds transfer.
MILES	where are you bro??
CRAZY E	you see this bloody shit, man? WTF
CAFÉ BLONDE	Running late?
JA JA	looks like Goldie lost his head. Let's talk.
MILES	WTF DONNIE?!?!

"Ugh," was his only response, tossing the phone back on the seat. He wheeled the car back onto El Camino Real, headed south towards the city, that glowing orange cloud looming over the mountain.

This is nuts, he thought. *Never ends.*

Donnie grabbed a small case from his jacket pocket and popped two little star-shaped blue pills into his mouth.

Getting too close to the ground.

He knocked back some water and focused on the steering wheel as the light turned green again. The horizon would grow sharper in a few moments and the world would flatten out for miles. The blue stars were his super-drug. Kept him alert, unemotional, quick on recall, and free.

Donnie called it *flying*.

This was his jam.

He flicked through the gears onto Interstate 5, his black chrome beast roaring into fifth. It was back to business and Donnie needed information. There was only one place in all of SD that stayed neutral and safe for all the clans. Always a guaranteed stock of drugs, connections, and information.

A place called Insomnia, open all hours.

NINE

KAL STUMBLED DOWN the sidewalk, seeing unfiltered with the Sight as the curse awoke his demons. Neon signs blazed like words of power in the midnight fog and reflected backwards in street puddles like the ancient names of gods. Car horns punctuated tires in the slick and the voice of Babylon rose like a chorus. The sky rolled overhead in a fast forward time lapse, dark clouds obscuring some molten red hell on the other side. Steam rose from the ground and swayed like the dance of spirits. Far away the screams of hunting and eating distorted the landscape.

Why was Kal Renley the Medicine Man? He wasn't so sure he knew anymore. He had dissolved his ego, his mind, his identity so many times with chemical benders and occult head trips, he didn't have much to cling to anymore. He was just this *thing* in the world. This agent of detox in a sick and bloated reality. Medicine Man. Witch Doctor. Conjure Man. Sin Eater.

They find him, these sick people, these poor souls possessed of spirits and curses. They find him and he doesn't have a choice but to help. It's in his nature, much as he might fight it. Align their frequency, cleanse their polluted spirit, maybe scare the hell right out of them. Either way, he had Vision and that's what people want, what they go out questing for.

But she was different, somehow.

Kal clutched his stomach and was violently sick. His almighty vision was only serving to torture and taunt him at the moment. He had to keep moving. Couldn't stop to look at the nightmare or indulge the little howlings. Just keep moving. Seeking. Thirsting.

Like a herald angel, the hanging sign to Jimmy's Pawn Shop swam out of the fog to announce the one place in the neighborhood that stocked a hidden cache of the Joos. Kal nearly threw himself at the door. A sickly bell announced his arrival as he toppled through the unlocked entrance with a resounding thud.

"What the hell?"

Startled voices and shuffling feet surrounded Kal as the world spun him upside down repeatedly.

"Goddamn tweekers, get him up!" bellowed a nasally voice Kal recognized.

Several hands pulled Kal to his feet and tossed him against the counter. The place was a funhouse of otherworldly nightmares, a place diseased and sick with predation and corruption. Exactly the place Kal wanted to put his magic tonic so he'd only seek it for emergencies. The posse of dirty thugs were Jimmy's guys and every single one of them was practically crawling with hell. They were soulless hustlers and, from his curse-induced Visions, Kal could see bugs crawling all over their faces, a telltale omen of a diseased soul. He looked away to steady himself.

"Who's dis fuckin' guy?"

"Ey you! Look at me ya piece o' shit!"

Kal looked up at the hustlers with infested faces and scowling eyes and mumbled, "Jimmy..."

It was enough to get their attention.

The face that came forward looked like it had been run over by a truck but the eyes said the guy didn't give two shits. They called him Jimmy the Spyder and this was his place. Pawn shop by day, drop off your junk until you can come back for it. After dark it was the hot spot for any substance outside the law. Percs, thiz, crank, mollies... whatever trips you take, the tickets are sold here beneath the orange canopy of a single grimy light bulb.

"Sweet baby Jesus, wouldja look who it is," Jimmy said with a wily grin smeared across that ugly mug of his. "The witch doctor himself."

Kal coughed up blood and pushed against the demonic droning in his ears to find focus.

"Jimmy..." he mumbled, lifting his head and suppressing the twitch in his lip. "Joos..."

The grogginess was setting in and Kal was getting twitchy, not to mention the visions all around him. A bobbing spirit-germ floated in his peripheral like a comet with legs and tentacles. Eyes stared out from the stacks of junk.

"Joos, huh?" Jimmy toyed with him as his boys got a good chuckle.

"You still have a vial or two," said Kal.

"Yeah. And whatchoo got, Doc?"

Kal eyed him. The bastard pulled this shit on the junkies and tweekers that fell into his little fly trap. His greasy posse got a good kick out of the petty power they dangled over the heads of addicts. The weak and desperate of the streets will fall at the feet of anyone. But Kal didn't have time for this shit. That curse was still swimming around in his gut like a hungry parasite, making it impossible to make words and he was about to succumb to the ravenous, evil hunger working its way through his veins.

The pawn shop monkeys were still laughing, still infested and sick with tall shadows creeping up the walls behind them. Kal saw it all.

"....What...I...got....?"

He relaxed and slumped against the glass counter, the sickness rising up in his throat, his energy field wavering and weak. It would all come crashing in any minute, he just needed a taste.

The left side of the world looked flat and glossy like a wall. And the right side was a cliff straight down. Reality narrowed to a 2D plane, a page on a screen.

Was this a pawn shop or a cliff of the abyss?

There it comes.

Kal felt it crawl up his windpipe slowly and with much oozing until a wrenching contortion sent him vomiting thick black tar onto the countertop.

It hissed and steamed as it ate through the glass surface and the jewelry inside.

Jimmy recoiled in disgust. "Damnit, man, what the fuck is—"

Jimmy's face contorted. Kal was buzzing. A twisting mask of shadows dipped over the Medicine Man's face and a sick, clawing feeling crept its way up Jimmy's throat.

"Cut it out," Jimmy warned with a choke. "Boys!"

His boys were busy pawing at their own throats like desperate, confused bears as Kal's sickness spread out across the shop.

All Kal had to do was drop back and let his otherworldly hunger become their hunger. His terror become their terror. Let them share what he was going through.

The thugs grew weak and fearful, had trouble breathing, and without knowing what was happening they began to see with the Sight. All the little nasties that lurk in the corners of their private hellhole glared at them from the shadows and reflections. Flying rats of the subconscious, floating parasites of the spirit. The clan that called themselves the Grunge Monkeys was now in screaming terror as they clawed at their eyes and stumbled around in panic. Only thing that stopped Kal from forming a satisfied grin was the horrible feeling working its way up his windpipe.

Kal gripped the counter to avoid falling over backward and it erupted. A bone-rattling moan from the underworld came up through his throat, dampening the air around them all with the sick, wet heat of torment as it washed a deafening tide of reverberation across the room. It buckled every knee in the building and Kal all but passed out from the vibrations.

"Alright, Doc, Alright!" Jimmy screamed, white as a sheet, hands in the air defensively. "Please!"

The witch doctor willed the sickness back into his swimming guts, wrestled it like a lanky Brazilian kick boxer until it was stuffed into the trap door of his mind, and the room went quiet. Jimmy stared at him a moment and then darted back into the stacks. The symptoms clawed at Kal's guts as he followed smartass Jimmy to the back, the pawn monkeys pawing at their throats behind him and looking around the shop in horrified confusion.

Jimmy wound through shelves of pawned artifacts from his addicted clientele to an old-fashioned wooden stereo speaker in the back corner. After a brief glance at the haunted psycho over his shoulder, Jimmy reached in the back of the speaker and withdrew two vials of gleaming, radiant red liquid.

Kal's eyes sparkled.

Come to Daddy...

"Last two," Jimmy said even as Kal snatched them hungrily from his grubby hands. Jimmy eyed the maniac, horrified that Kal might explode at any moment. Kal kept his greedy, needy, beady little eyes on the vial of sweet nectar, the yearning in his blood coming to a boil.

No more hesitation, he turned and clawed his way out of the shop, bringing down an iron shelf of old typewriters and broken laptops with a misplaced stumble. Then he was out onto the howling street.

Joos...

Sweet sweet medicine...

Like most tonics he trafficked, the Joos was something Kal made himself. His own private alchemical heaven that had its own steep price. It had a way of becoming a problem. Not like opiates or tryptamines, no the Joos was something in a category all its own. Laced with lysergic peptides and a compound known as Godsbane, he brewed it only on the Equinoxes and sweetened it with fruit juice. Had a mind of its own, that stuff, so he kept emergency stashes hidden around the city for his own good. But it was the only thing that could rescue him from the more powerful demons and curses of the world.

Kal stumbled down the alley behind the pawn shop, shaky hands fumbling anxiously with the stopper until he finally popped it off and released the sweet smell of some faraway place.

Fuck. Yes. I need it... he's thinking to himself. *God, I need it.*

He dumped a blot into each eye, the red streaming down his cheeks like some weeping stigmata then gulped down the rest of the vial. He didn't even hear the footsteps approaching from the side. Didn't smell the cheap perfume she wore or the black magic she carried.

She found him there somehow and as the witch doctor swayed and dropped to his knees, the Joos already sliding through his bloodstream, he looked up at her from far away. She stood there watching as his eyes glossed over and the chimes of Infinity came rushing through his inner ears, sweeping away the torment of the Underworld. He collapsed against the cold brick and let it in, the wash of relief, the overflow of neurochemical spirit that simultaneously cleansed and polluted his soul.

Little chemical building blocks of peace to quiet the screams of hell and the angels' trumpets.

Trumpets...

"I can't stay," she says.

How'd you find me?

He's not actually saying it, only thinking it, because his tongue is the size of a bullfrog and all he can do is make gurgling sounds.

Will you do it?

"Will you?" her cracked lips and eyes the size of space stations hover inches away in blurry watercolor, and Kalvin Renley tells her *Yes*.

Her face is the night sky, that glint in her eye the moon, and from somewhere far away as he slips and falls with the Joos, he tells Eden he'll fix her.

I'll fix you.

"I can't stay," she says and they're both gone.

TEN

THE ICONIC BLACK JAGUAR roared to a stop at the curb outside a place called Insomnia.

North County clans called it Mecca. The club lived on the main drag in Pacific Beach, a two story structure that looked like a glass house full of icy blue light. Searchlights roamed the sky overhead and the whole neighborhood felt the steady beat that rolled from the open doors. A line of the city's night life bourgeoisie wrapped around the building inside crimson ropes under the watchful eye of an Armani suit security detail. Everyone with any ties to the Game could be found inside those walls on a good night.

Donnie smoothed his hair in the rear view mirror. He knew how this worked. The crowd was already loud and anxious. Athen's club had always been the center of the scene, headquarters and nexus of the Game. Lights, phones, crowd. You had to put on a show, which was alright by Donnie, except tonight he was here on sensitive business.

He stepped out and handed his keys to a valet who nodded with respect. Heads turned up and down the sidewalk and Donnie tried not to flinch, silver briefcase worth 20 years in prison gripped casually in hand. No one would dare mess with him here but you could never be too sure anymore. Deep breath. He was a charismatic asshole, sure, but spotlights made Donnie uncomfortable. His eyes focused on the doors, the kingpin made a series of long strides to the top of the red carpeted staircase and gave a nod to the two guys working the door in stark white tailored suits.

"Mr. DeGrassi," the first man said with a nod of respect. His associate unclipped the velvet rope to let Donnie through.

Muttering his thanks, Donnie caught sight of a girl standing near the front of the line. She was a gorgeous brunette done up in a silver dress and she was giving him serious eyes. Donnie nodded in her direction and Security let her through.

She blushed and smiled at Donnie. He was about half paying attention. It was more for the show.

The inside crowd only. Athen, the shyster who owned the joint, liked to keep it exclusive because, of course, that's what made it cool. Didn't hurt that he made sure everyone inside was a buyer or a seller. In those games, the house always wins.

"You a vodka girl?"

"Tequila all the way," she replied.

Big surprise there.

Donnie gave the guards an appreciative nod and made his way through the cold vapor that sprayed the air at the doors of Insomnia, the only blue-beamed ice house on the coast.

There are worse things to do for a living, he thought to himself.

Insomnia's marble floor wrapped around an open arena pit that looked like it was carved out of ice. Blue hues and colored lights refracted through the fully open three story ceiling. Top shelf liquors at a bar to the left, plush furniture and added privacy in the lounge to the right. The arena pit in the middle of the room hosted a dance floor that raged and thumped like a living thing, all smoke and sweat and movement curled up at the base of a DJ podium that rose above the crowd like sculpted ice.

Higher still was a circular enclosed balcony where the lighting glowed green inside and silhouettes leaped from side to side like shadows. Way up there, in that nest over the party, that was Athen's little VIP suite where he conducted business and kept watch from on high. His throne above the palace.

"This is great!" shouted Tequila Girl over the music.

Donnie nodded and made a beeline for the bar. He needed a drink before diving into the mountains of bullshit and intrigue Insomnia could serve up on a good night.

The bar wrapped a wide arc around the left side of the club and Donnie had his favorite spot. It was like sitting at a block of ice to have a drink, complete with the vapor sliding across its surface. Bar staff all dressed in white leather outfits of varied outlandishness and not a damn one of them looked the worse for it.

"Long time no see, handsome," greeted a red-haired bartender a few years Donnie's senior.

"How's business, Wanda?"

"Every asshole for twenty miles is here testing my patience, how d'you think it is?"

Donnie smiled.

"Shot of crown. Tequila for the lady."

"Who's your friend?"

Donnie shrugged and turned to survey the room while Wanda winked at Tequila Girl and bustled off to pour the poison. A quick sweep of the scene and he was surprised. Surely the East County incident would have scared most of the clans away, made the place a ghost town of desperate tourists. But no, Athen was much too good for that, too obsessed with his fame and his *brand*. No amount of the ultra-violence would get in the way of his spectacle.

The clans were out in force. Representatives from every tribe and every turf were mingling in a posh, snazzy atmosphere of neon light and heavy bass. They all wanted to know what was going on, what would happen next, and how they could benefit. Patch update in the game and everyone's ready to level up.

"What do we drink to?"

Donnie's attention returned to the smiling slim dress and the shot of whiskey waiting for him.

At the clink of the glass, he gave her a grin. "To the game."

Tequila wasn't sure what that meant but she threw the shot back anyway.

Donnie knocked back the whiskey knowing it would explode like wildfire when it mixed with the flight caps in his bloodstream. Extra fuel. He scanned the room as the burn reached his stomach and the wide horizon started to glow hot. They were all here.

Insomnia was like an oasis for the soul starved. The dancing, the drinks, the conversations, all of it had something to do with the illicit trade of one chemical or another. Some took you on a bender to the outer planets and back, others got you high as a kite and dropped you hard. There were hallucinations in Hyper-Pixar Technicolor and dazzling orgies of eccentric sensations produced by pills, tabs, drops, drinks, and powders. Reality blurred and melted depending on what was in your blood and on the screens and in your head. Oxygen was piped into the air to give the whole crowd a perpetual levitation and everyone there would admit to feeling on top of the world.

Drugs were hot in southern Cali in this strange new time out of time with all the raw data in the air and screens in the peoples' hands. San Diego was a port for the mass exodus of seekers reaching for exit portals to new worlds and wild rides, looking for answers and frontiers. But the shifting landscape of control clans and tryptamine tribes was an entirely different beast.   Anyone could be a producer or a distributor, and everyone was a potential buyer. You made your own rules, so long as they fit into the bigger rules.

Newbies were met with the typical feeler question, "What kinda vibe you chasin'?"

From there a host of delicacies was suggested for consumption. It was trashy and it was decadent and Donnie ate that shit up. This was his gig.

The usual suspects were all here, each working an angle. Each with an agenda.

Athen's boys were the ones in white, moving through the throngs of high class revelers with trays of drinks and pockets full of designer drugs.

Ace the Snake had a table in the back corner where he entertained out-of-town clients and worked people for risky favors.

Ja Ja Le Rue was the queen of the Diva Saints who turned their little massage brothel into a clan of skilled thieves and subtle assassins for sale to the highest bidder.

The Frostheads, The Bolly Bakers, and the Rag Tag Flog Flag were all exchanging hits of the latest vape potions and mingling amongst themselves. Reps from the Taggerts and Buzzheads kept their distance and eyed the others. Old hats from the Thirteen Kings took up the big booth in the far corner.

Place was a who's who of the scene, all of them out for a jump on the rest.

The new kid everyone was calling Bubz strutted around making plays for bigger action and most likely far too caught up in the glitz and glamour to avoid biting off more than he could chew.

The list went on and on, a flourishing underworld of tribal decadence and underhanded alliances. And it's not like there weren't consequences. The Feds still watched the market and regularly put people in cages for possession and trafficking. Tension was always a factor and eccentric trypsters could be... *eccentric.* The tapestry of the trade was only loosely held in place by the Pax, a kind of trust that was formed when Kal's next gen meds hit the market. For a while things just kinda cruised along, even after Kal snapped and disappeared.

Until someone crossed a serious line.

"Fuckin' A, Donnie!"

Donnie savored the burn of the chemical cocktail flowing through his veins as a wild-haired Miles collapsed onto the stool next to him.

"Whad'ya say, Miles," Donnie grumbled through the burn.

"Donnie, this is fucked," said Miles looking paranoid and unrested. "Totally fucked."

"You worry too much."

"You don't worry enough, Donnie!" Miles ran his hands through his hair and across his sweat-soaked face. "Seven—! Seven bodies, Donnie, seven motherfu—"

"Whoa whoa, easy, kid," Donnie said, putting a calming hand on his buddy and looking around to make sure he wasn't freaking out any nearby eavesdroppers. "Take it easy. I'm on this, alright?"

Donnie nodded for a shot and Wanda brought it over.

"I'm right in the middle, Donnie," Miles said, shaking. He sipped the whiskey slowly.

"I know, Miles, I know."

The guy had a right to be a little on edge and Donnie knew it. Miles was the point man between the East Side Locos and the Krank Street Krew. Whoever gunned down the Locos would likely come for him next and if they didn't, one of the Kranks would be looking to put him through some *enthusiastic* questioning.

A quick glance confirmed Tequila Girl had gotten bored and wandered off. Just as well. Donnie leaned in close to Miles.

"This is too big a deal to start runnin' around all bat shit crazy, right?" he whispered. "Let me do the digging. We'll see what's goin' on and what these clowns are up to. In the meantime, why don't you head back to my apartment and get some sleep. You look like shit, Miles."

Miles finished his drink and nodded.

"Thanks, Donnie."

Donnie gave Miles a pat on the back and ordered two more shots.

"Donnie, hey-Donnie, sorry, hey," mumbled a scrawny kid in an oversized hoodie. "Did you talk to him?"

"What?"

"The Medicine Man, did you talk to him?"

Donnie smirked and finished his drink. What was he supposed to say? *Yeah kid he's hiding in his house on a perpetual balls-tripping bender talking nonsense to himself. Want him to bake you a fucking cake?*

"No, Marvin," is what he actually says. "Nobody has."

He never got used to that look of doubt and lost hope that crept over them when he gave that answer. Marvin wandered off to nurse his disappointment. Moments like those, flying around in the past, he wondered if they had done the right thing.

The streets always had gangs and turf wars but it was The Game that changed it all. Heightened it, brought things to the next level. The digital network connected people into strange little clans and tribes as they partook of a plethora of new psychic substances. Kal was kicking up new compounds every week and sending people into the hyper levels of outer space and time. He was healing people and bringing them to life. Folks were getting to strange worlds and levels of consciousness, bizarre little mind connections formed, the world got a lot more colorful and complicated.

Immediately there were tribes and clans and lines in the sand. Fights over style and niche and psychic turf. A kind of tribal zealotry over reality. Wars on the unseen playground. Mind, symbol, technology, chemicals, near-telepathic communication mixed with complex thought patterns in the mind.

People went crazy in mass.

The kind of crazy that has them gyrating and posturing in a dreamhouse called Insomnia at three in the morning. Eventually things got out of hand and drove Kal out of the game. Now it had come to this.

On cue, a bald-headed man in a white suit approached Donnie from behind.

"He will see you now."

Donnie had to hand it to Athen. Guy had a way with theatrics. Donnie knocked back the shot and followed Mr. Clean to the winding staircase that ascended to the presence of His Royal Highness.

The stairs to Athen's nest wound in a large arc around the entire club so that it took some time to get up there. Athen made sure you had to see the whole place on your way up to his throne.

They reached the plush loft to find the man of the house seated on an *actual* throne, some gaudy absurdity of a chair, surrounded by a smattering of Abercrombie models on fluffy pillows and a squad of stoic body builders in tailored white suits.

"Athen," Donnie nodded.

"Donnie De-fucking-Grassi."

The Hipster King reclined in his seat of power, sending a few texts from a holographic screen that floated over the arm of his chair. Donnie never seen anything like it. Athen stood as Donnie entered.

He wore a skinny suit trimmed artfully and colored to match the environment he had crafted around him. Athen was a thin wraith, all bones and pale flesh, and sported a twisty little chin beard the color of blue icing and round spectacles tinted Coca Cola red. Poster child for the bold audacity of a brave new Millennium.

Athen helped himself to one of those friendly two-pat hugs knowing it would make Donnie uncomfortable. Donnie shook him off and moved to a spot at the private bar. The angelic models winked and beckoned at him and he ignored every bit of it.

"I see you're doin' alright," Athen said, sliding onto one of the blue leather barstools.

Donnie laid his silver briefcase on the counter and shrugged. "Never a dull moment."

Athen appreciated the brooding wit as Donnie popped the lid of the case open to reveal twenty generic pill bottles with no labels. Each was full of little white tablets of pure MDMA, stamped with the signature smiley face.

"Ah, tickets to the Love Boat," Athen said with a poetic sigh and a hand over his heart. He motioned for Mr. Clean to take the case while he grabbed two tumblers from the bar. The bodyguard traded Donnie a small silver cigarette case that housed a plastic bank card.

Donnie slid it into his jacket pocket and stepped away from the case of molly. The bald headed beefcake promptly left the room with the case.

Athen finished pouring and offered Donnie a celebratory drink.

"To the Game," they both quoted.

Their glasses clinked and the Johnny Walker washed into their bellies. Donnie was feeling the buzz but he was still flying. The world was still that chess board a million miles wide. Figured this put him at least even with the sly snake at the top of Insomnia.

Any minute now he'd make his move on—

"How's our friend the magic medicine man doing, eh, Donnie?"

Like clockwork.

"Kal's a hermit these days," Donnie responded lazily. Set the glass on the counter and straightened his shirt cuffs.

"I'm sure he finds time amongst his surfing and sleeping to brew up the goods," Athen prodded.

"Hardly finds it in him to brew up a shower."

"I see. Well, all the same, tell him I want the old stuff. Bananza, Golden Shief, even the Joos he claimed was revolutionary in our time. I want it all back on the market, Donnie. I'll do whatever I have to."

"You know how he is."

"All too well," Athen grinned. "Which is why you have to get him to Res Fest this weekend."

Donnie almost forgot about Athen's big desert rave. The guy had been raining promo cards and graffiti on the city for weeks and he made sure it stayed trending on all the web feeds. Half music festival, half psychedelic extravaganza, Res Fest was Athen's dream project finally come to life.

"Figured you'd cancel considering what happened to the Locos," said Donnie with a challenging sniff.

Athen looked offended. Got him by surprise.

"I heard about that," said Athen. "Fucking meta, right? But the show must go on, Donnie. Besides, do you know how much I've already put into this? It's unsettling. It unsettles me, Donnie. I am unsettled."

"A gang hit snapping seven heads unsettles all of us, Athen."

"All part of the game, buddy," Athen muttered and returned to his throne with the glowing chat screen floating like a hologram above his hands.

Donnie watched him with a sneer. Little shit liked to pick his battles and for this one he had his tail between his legs.

The blank-stare models draped around the room all beckoned Donnie's attention, undulating bodies layered over one another, a constant temptation, a never-ending intoxication.

"You do business in TJ?" he asked, focusing his attention (and mounting frustration) on Athen.

"I do business wherever I have to," Athen replied smugly, not looking up from his texting.

It had been a long night for Donnie and he was about five shots of whiskey into Insomnia's bullshit. It was almost a reflex. Before the thoughts registered way up there at Blue Star altitude, his hand had already twitched and pulled out the gun. His finger had already squeezed. The rage was like a tick and suddenly Athen's chair arm exploded into shrapnel, the gunshot getting lost in the thumping bass from downstairs.

"Jesus Christ, Donnie!" Athen said leaping back from the blast.

They both froze in the fallout. The shot had been aimed at the phone deck—that bizarre little hologram Athen felt was so much more important than their conversation— and it certainly put a stop to the texting. But by taking out the computer, Donnie had shut off another hologram program that had been running unnoticed in the room. The girls, the guards, the whole lavish entourage that made Athen a god, it flickered and went out like a dying light. The room was empty.

Donnie stared at Athen a long time and, for once, the little asshole didn't know what to say.

"Smoke and mirrors," Donnie whispered.

"You have my fucking attention," Athen said, the irritation simmering off of him, his Supreme Cool melting like hot ice.

"What do you know about Oblivion?"

Athen got serious and turned a dagger stare on Donnie.

"You got a funny way of asking for favors, DeGrassi."

Donnie realized he still had the gun in his hand. He holstered it behind his back, straightened his shirt, and regained his composure.

Athen waved the question away.   "Lot of rumors, of course. Ruthless rancheros drumming up Santeria and old world curses. Killing their rivals. Eyes set on our market. Hard to believe these gun-toting badasses are so stupidly superstitious but then I remind myself of our friend Kal's little... gifts."

"Santeria?" Donnie raised an eyebrow. "The Catholic stuff?"

"Older, I'm sure," said Athen. "I don't know, man. It's all hocus pocus to me. But it's scaring the right people."

"Which exactly? Who put Goldie and the Locos under the gun, A?"

Athen seemed small in his over-sized chair, cowering before Donnie without his false posse of digital friends. This was the miserable whelp Donnie remembered from back in the day, back when they were all hustling for chump change and Insomnia was just a dream. Kid got soft.

"Who, Athen?!"

"I don't know, D!" Athen admitted. "Last I heard Goldie was running this Oblivion stuff for el Brujan. Told him to get me some but that was more than a week ago. Hadn't heard from him."

"Who's Xechan?" Donnie asked, most important question saved for last.

"They call him—"

"Yeah, I know his nickname. Who is he really?"

"Best I can figure, Donnie, he's a hungry upstart with just enough balls and crazy to be dangerous," Athen said as serious as he'd been all night. "Like a few others I've come to know."

Donnie watched out the tinted walls of their perch as the club lights shifted blood red and the bass dropped low beneath his feet.

"Who else has contact with 'em?"

Athen thought for a minute. "Only one other guy besides Goldie but he got picked up in the last raid out in Julian."

Donnie ran through the guys he knew had been caged. "Bosley?"

Athen nodded. "Anything else, officer?"

That was all he needed. "Be seeing you, A. Your secret's safe with me."

Donnie left Insomnia's Master of Ceremonies to his empty room.

"Careful out there," Athen warned. "The Game has changed."

"So have we," grumbled Donnie.

It was no surprise that Bone-Knuckle Bosley was the other idiot just stupid enough to make deals with the devil. The guy was some kind of satanic lunatic who ran some off-shoot chapter of the Hell's Angels in east county. He crossed too many lines and the other clans turned him in. Cops got him and eight other guys that day. Donnie's insider at the DEA had told him they had found something new in their blood after detox but they never figured out what it was. Must have been the cartel's first try.

If Bosley had answers, he'd have to visit him in lockdown.

Donnie couldn't help but snigger at Athen's dirty little tricks as he descended from the perch. All this illusion to hide one little twerp's insecurities. Donnie felt like he'd been waging war all night. Whiskey had him loose and chewing at his own teeth, the oxygen in the air had him light-headed. Like coming down from a trip, he stepped out to the quiet street and the smell of the ocean as a valet went to retrieve the Jag.

Donnie's thumbs punched at his iPhone.

TO: BIANCA   omw

He pocketed the phone and ducked into the sports car as the eastern sky was starting to see the first pale blue of dawn

ELEVEN

MILES WALKED ALONG the empty sidewalks of the Gaslamp District on his way to Donnie's condo. Insomnia's buzz had worn off and all that was left was the fear. They could be gunning for him, any of them. Those brutal bastards could be holding a gun or a lit match around any corner.

He turned up a side street and heard his name.

"Hey Miles!"

Miles nearly jumped out of his skin.

"Oh, hey Marshall," he sighed in relief at the site of one of his loyal customers. "Whatcha doing out here?"

"Waiting on a delivery," Marshall said with a grin and an anxious twitch. Had a friend behind him, squirrely little guy with giant ears. Miles knew Marshall from the kid's days running for the D Town Dogs. Hustled meth and pills mostly. Small time, old school stuff.

"Right," Miles mumbled, moving along. "Be careful out here."

Terrible things in the night these days.

"Yeah, you too man."

Miles made it to the other end of the block before Marshall's contact came zipping up on a skateboard.

"Bout time," Marshall said with a playful grin.

The guy they called Wheelz unstrapped his helmet and reached into his canvas shoulder bag. No greetings or small talk, just handed over a taped manila package.

"Awesome," Marshall said, handing over a wad of cash.

Something was different about this guy Wheelz. His eyes were dark and smoky, had this kind of far-out glassy shine to them.

"You rollin' on something, bro?" asked Marshall.

Wheelz just nodded and pulled out a second package. Little plastic baggie with a small amount of black powder inside.

Marshall and his curious friend were mesmerized.

"What's this?"

"Next evolution," was the cryptic answer from Wheelz.

"Like medicine man stuff?"

"Better."

"Better?"

"There's a new game in town," said Wheelz.

Marshall took the baggie and looked at its contents. Opened the bag and inhaled. Just the smell of this stuff gave him an immediate buzz and tingle. His eyes lit up.

"How much?"

Wheelz revealed a creepy, dazed grin. "It's a sample. Enjoy."

With that, Wheelz strapped his helmet and took off on the skateboard.

Marshall and his buddy exchanged looks of intrigue and excitement. Without further hesitation, Marshall took a pinch and snuffed it.

Miles watched from his alcove at the end of the block, trembling in fear. He knew what that was and who had given it to them. Didn't take long for Marshall to start stumbling around and freaking out. Kid grabbed at his eyes and screamed, frightening his friend who dropped the manila package and backed away.

"Marshall?" the friend tried but now Marshall was already on the ground, rolling and twisting in terror and screaming out into the night.

"Oh god..." Miles whispered.

"Hardly," responded a voice over his shoulder.

Miles swung around in surprise to find a trio of dark figures. The first was a sharp man in a tailored black suit and red sunglasses. His angular face sported an amused expression and behind him stood two of the bone-masked soldiers of el Brujan. Miles backed up into the wall and his heart thundered the drums of flight.

"What do you—?"

85

"Let's not be coy," hissed the devil's lieutenant. "This is the part where it gets fun."

Miles turned and sprinted down the sidewalk, tears on his face and a desperation in his breath. It was no use. The soldiers were in front of him like lightning and before he could even scream Miles had a bag over his head. The roar of a vehicle pulled up beside him and he was tossed unceremoniously into the darkness of the trunk.

Brujan Lieutenant Bael stayed behind as the vehicle sped off into the night. He was watching Marshall's motionless, unconscious body lying on the sidewalk.

It took a few minutes in the quiet night.

But the body started to twitch.

First the fingers, then the legs. Marshall clumsily found his footing and when he stood to his full height, Bael smiled. That was no burn-out from the streets. That was a new recruit.

Marshall's eyes had rolled completely back into his head and drool seeped from his mouth. There was a mindless shuffle to his walk and the smell of death upon him. The new recruit shuffled off into the night carrying the curse of Oblivion through the streets.

Bael sent a text from his mobile.

To: FC   Progress.

TWELVE

KAL KNEW HE was dreaming again.

One of those running down long hallways dreams. The sprint down the near-endless corridor ended at a red door that opened to a cliff's ledge when he burst through. Caught his balance as the door slammed close behind him. Locked him out there on the edge, overlooking the empty valley of what used to be San Diego.

Used to be.

No more palm trees, no more reggae, no more lights in the night.

All he saw was fire for miles. A burning desert of anguish.

He saw them like a mob. A frenzied, disgusting herd of ravenous hands and mouths, all reaching for his molecules, greedy for his medicine.

Bubbling, frothy red Joos that washed away the sin and opened up the grimy windows of Spirit.

They abuse it. They don't want health or transformation, they lust for the trip, the high, the buzz. Chasing only dopamine and serotonin, they don't get it.

And why should they?

They don't want the vision. The burden of truth.

They're grabbing greedily at the drugs like animals.

Dead head zombies.

Monsters.

These were the monsters he created.

The Medicine Man's ravenous army.

His own sins reaching back for him. Clawing at his feet. Climbing up to rip him apart.

The sun swelled to a red fruit in the sky. At the sound of a Great Gong in the distance the blazing sky tyrant exploded into a supernova of blood that rained down on the sea of raging fists and the world was set to drown in its own sacrifice.

KAL WOKE TO the quibbling of pigeons in the back alley of Jimmy's Pawn Shop. His body felt like he'd been packed through a garbage truck, hangover swinging from his head like an anvil. Picked himself up from the warm pavement like some hobo and greeted a new day. The glass clink sound of a vial rolling across the pavement reminded him he Joosed last night. Then a voice snuck up on him.

"It's almost time."

Kal looked around for the speaker but he was alone in the sun bleached alley.

"Almost time," said the stranger again.

This time Kal saw it, just a few feet away.

"Time, time, almost time," the creature said again, cocking his head sideways to take in the sight of this back alley addict. Kal pinched the bridge of his nose and steadied himself.

The speaker wasn't a person but a street pigeon. A *talking* street pigeon. Kal tried not to look at it. Tried to separate the hallucinations from the material. Tried to ground himself in *the real* but reality had all but abandoned him long ago. Yes, that filthy bird was speaking and damn unfortunate it was too because these city vermin always foretold doom and gloom.

"Time for what?" Kal asked.

The little harbinger cocked its head again and returned to picking at random bits of garbage, inert as any dumb animal. (These things come and go.) Kal picked himself up and brushed off his clothes. The sun was just now rising over the city.

Bright sunlight scorched Kal's sensitive eyes and he fumbled for the shades in his jacket pocket. They were pretty slick aviators at one time, now scuffed and scratched with a bent arm and a missing nose pad but they served him well. Shielded his eyes from the UV rays and shielded others from his eyes. Folks don't take kindly to the insane leer of a spirit conjurer fresh off hell's bender.

Kal brushed himself off and tried to orient to the day. He'd been cursed last night just by looking unprepared at an inked tattoo. After all the summoning he'd done to make that tonic for the sick girl, he was drained when the thing blasted him. Invaded him. Made his skin crawl just thinking about it. That and the Joos hangover had him in quite a state. Headache, tight jaw, dry sensitive eyes, and acid flashbacks where the spirit world bleeds through. The price you pay for the good stuff.

And that girl. Said her name was Eden. She'd gotten into some nasty stuff and then Kal scared her away. The gods only knew where she was now. Well, maybe them and—

"Meklyn!" Kal suddenly called out, pairing his voice with a booming echo in his mind, a sounding call for his otherworldly pet. Almost before he formed the word, the winged little rat appeared on his shoulder in a fit of sparks.

Immediately Meklyn screeched in a shrill goblin pitch, the sun's rays scorching his spectral body. Kal stepped into the shade to shield him. The creature squinted his swirling red orbs and showed a mouthful of gritted, pointy teeth. In the daylight he was harder to see, his form more translucent, like a distorted shape in the scenery.

"Stupid wakeup calls," Meklyn grunted, holding up a hand to block the light from his eyes. Little thing always had attitude after Kal Joosed. The trip shook up the subconscious where the creature slept.

"You'd prefer a summoning triangle?" Kal mused.

Meklyn was Kal's own creation, a cross between mind and matter bonded to him with Kal's own blood. What some would call a *homunculus* or a *servitor*, Meklyn was a creature of Kal's own flesh and psyche. A supernatural psycho-magical familiar, an extension of Kal's power, and a spirit of the under-realms where he communicated with his master's DNA, manipulated subtle energy fields, and scoured the collective unconscious. The latter was today's reason for calling.

"The girl," Meklyn gathered immediately.

"Can you find her?"

Kal saw the imp's bloodpool eyes shimmer as he looked into the underworld, the bloodstream and under-consciousness of everyone with whom Kal had ever come in contact.

"Shifty," groaned the creature.

"Just look," Kal muttered.

"I'll think about it."

And *POOF*, just like that, he was gone.

Shaking off the grogginess and squinting into the bright light of California day, Kal made his way through town. He didn't bother looking back as he put space between himself and Jimmy's Pawn Shop. He already knew where to go next.

THIRTEEN

THE SHADOW OF A BIRD fell over sun-baked red brick to the sound of a shaking aerosol can. A liquid mist of blood red paint spewed across the brick in large sweeping arcs. The bird shadow flapped its wings.

"The sun god, Quetzalcoatl, is the shape of time itself," said a voice.

The bird shadow—fashioned by a set of hands—flapped once again over the red circle of fresh paint. A wet swollen sun on the wall.

"His face comes around again every rotation, every sun, to reset the world mind."

The speaker made a sad attempt at a bird sound.

Then silence.

"The air tastes like candy," whispered someone else and a trio of voices broke into hooting laughter.

The Witness Boys left the paint to dry on the wall, streaks of red dripping down the warm brick surface, and returned to their perch. Tripps, Davie, and Kiefer held their vigil most mornings at the water tower overlooking Spring Valley.   Empty spray paint canisters and crushed green tea cans lay strewn about the hilltop among the rocks as lingering evidence of their morning rituals. They were dressed in baggy skater punk clothes that hung loose on their skinny forms with identical round sunglasses over their eyes, each a different color.

While most people took them for stoners and high-school dropouts—which they were—Kal knew them as friends, allies, and pseudo prophets.   They had strange ways but their predictions almost always proved accurate. (From most points of view.)

"Right where I left ya," said Kal from the foot path.

His voice drew their attention and the boys looked up in unison, their round shades like six reflective eyes at some alien pow-wow.

"Kal?" Kiefer said, lowering his shades and squinting.

"No shit," Davie muttered.

"The prodigal son returns," chimed Tripps.

Kal joined his buddies on the rocks, tossing a can of Arizona Green Tea to each of them as his offering to the oracles. The boys were pretty specific about their preferred beverage. The gift was met with approving smiles and thirsty groans.

"Where you been, Doc?" Kiefer asked, cracking his can.

"Been a while," said Kal, leaning against the brick wall and admiring the sun sigil painted there. "I been a little far out."

"Off the fuckin' grid, you mean," said Kiefer. "You know how many people been asking about you?"

Kal had uncomfortable flashes of his Joos nightmare. Hands reaching from extended gutters for something to save them from their own sin and misery, molecules to release them from the prison of the self. But he was on a mountain now with the Witness Boys, far away from the herd and his Joos-fueled nightmares.

"Truth is, I need some help," he said.

"We know," the trio intoned in unison.

Kiefer slapped Kal on the back. "Came to the right place, brother."

The boys downed the rest of their drinks, crushed the cans, and tossed them aside where they piled up with the rest of the mountain's debris.

"You three look to be doing alright."

"The game ain't been the same since you left," said Keifer.

Davie nodded. "So we stay out of it."

Tripps brushed off his hands. "First thing's first."

The boys surrounded Kal and six hands spun him around to a seated spot on a large boulder facing the morning sun.

"Time to pray," said Tripps, plopping down shoulder-to-shoulder with Kal.

That was what the Witness Boys did after all, and so they set to work.

Davie strummed out a little ditty on his polished acoustic guitar while Tripps fumbled with a stash of sticky grass he pulled from one the many pockets in his patched jeans. Kiefer roamed around them, muttering some mantra to himself and waving his hands at the *genus loci* of the mountain.

Kal relaxed and watched. He was the go-to guy for magic and ritual but when it came to communion and prophecy, he liked to outsource. Even witch doctors seek the council of their peers in tough times and Kal trusted the good nature and innocence of this young trifecta more than anybody else.

"Ooh! Oy!" went the hoots directed at the flaming sun overhead.

Kal felt the electric charge building up in the air around them and relaxed his mind for what was to come. Tripps finished his concentrated work on the sacred communal herb and passed the expertly-twisted spliff to Kal.

Kal accepted the toke and hit it several times in succession, the quick, easy pulls of a pro. He passed it along to Davie and settled into the buzz to let the sun warm his face.

For some, Holy Communion is wine and wafers. For others it's the Creator's flowering stalks.

The toke came back around and Kal imbibed. Higher now...

Even the apostles partook of the plant and the Pharisees before them practically bathed in Cannabis oil. They called it 'getting in the spirit of the Lord.' These thoughts and others came easily to Kal as he relaxed. Kiefer fumbled with his smartphone until it started spewing an electronic beat to accompany Davie's song.

Kal looked over at Tripps, dazed out at the sight of the morning sun warm on his face and the peace of the air above the world. He met Kal's red-eyed gaze.

"High there," said Tripps and he fell into a joyful fit of stoned giggling.

Most people who smoke the sacred herb are easy fast food for the plant spirits. They get zapped and fried and maybe wander down the rabbit hole before returning to mow down some Cheetos.

But a medicine man understands the plant as a teacher and a tool. A life form millions of years older than humanity, an emissary from a different kingdom, it warmed the muscles and relaxed the tight boundaries of consciousness. The plant spoke, you just had to listen. Kal placed a hand over his heart, buzzing head to toe with little green symbols floating up into the air around him.

"Home," he whispered.

That was Kiefer's cue to start channeling.

He wandered around them shaking his hands at the Earth and lolling his head back and forth, spinning up a deep trance in time to the electro-beat. He paced a boundary of energy and mind around them all and when it was closed and charging, he opened his mouth to let the words out.

> "The sun rose red this morning and an eagle
> flew over the face.
> Face.
> Face like the Father, Holy Spirit in the photons,
> beams, bumpers, bumble berry bugaloo,
> the Great Eye Nebula in the Deep..."

He spit the words like poetry to accompany Davie's guitar ditties. Threw in little finger snaps and belly slaps as he paced back and forth.

> "A deep vine splintered
> deep deep deep beneath the city last night
> and the aliens from Sirius beamed him up.
> The invasion. The invader. The turning of the wheel.
> War sends the ambassadors running back to their
> bunkers,
> cash for clunkers...
> rummaging junkers...
> subconscious spelunkers..."

Kal let the bizarre babble wash over him. It was a trance Kiefer entered and it did you no good to approach his words with straight logic. He was channeling messages from higher realms and from deep in his own soul. You had to treat it like hidden layers of meaning in a song, be open to possibilities.

> "The healer returns in need of healing
> and his haunted soul has questions.
> Questions Answers Questions Answers,
> Q and A and Q and A
> Q! A!"

He worked himself into a kind of frenzy, a spastic fit, and then shouted, "Great Ones!"

"Great ones," Tripps echoed. "Hallelujah."

Kiefer's arms reached to embrace the whole sun. Kal was feeling it too. The music, the words, and Tripps always had Grade A Ganja. They were in the spin.

"Great ones. Ones of great. Ones and zeroes into
infinity...
Inifitismo, inifinitas, infinitum!
When the dead heads walk and the sky opens up, the
demon will speak, terrible terrible things spoken in ink
and flesh and dust--"

Thoughts and visions lapped against Kal's mind like a morning
tide. Surfing old waves, the old days, the Pax. Now he was alone in
darkness staring at a terrified set of beautiful brown eyes as an ink
leviathan wrapped its jagged tentacles around his subconscious and
pulled him down.

"Yes that," Kal mumbled. "The demon."

Kiefer repeated and stuttered the words a few times, "Demons,
demiurge, Demi Moore, demon-devil, tiny nasty howlings in the twisted
tattoo of her soul..." After the reverberating chorus in his flow he was
off on his own again.

"The beast has a vendetta, a mission for the flesh.
She waves her many arms and invites him to the party.
A devil squatting on Kim Kardashian's ass
and trumpets blasting MegaDeath.
The girl with the demon tattoo looks into the healer's
soul
and sees salvation."

Kal let thoughts and visions of Eden come to him and he saw
that horrible sigil.

"The dead of soul will walk the dust,
and Persephone is lost.

> Oblivion's Gate calls all to the 8th passage to darkness
> and it spreads like black mold in the—"

"Who?" Kal nearly leaped to his feet. "Who's work? Who's spell?"

> "They are the dark acolytes of death's return,
> Resurrection of old vanquished gods,
> Soul of the world caked in coal.
> He will raise his undead army and they will watch,
> The war pigs, the Masters,
> from on high as chaos and poison
> open the 8th Gate to Armageddon."

"Wait!" shouted Kal.

Silence.

Tuned into the same frequency, his mind had been spinning up visuals to accompany Kiefer's words. The undead armies and death gods along with sex, drugs, and Armageddon was enough for him to finally pull the air brake on this trip.

"Brujan," he said.

Kiefer stopped and looked at him. "Dude. You ruined my flow."

"The new drug," Kal said. "The bad medicine, what is it?"

"Oblivion," said Tripps.

"Demon dust," Kiefer said with a twitch, the trance still working fits in him.

"You know it?"

Tripps grinned and Kal saw himself in those red reflective lenses. "I know 'em all, brother."

"Tell me."

Kiefer wandered in a circle and sat down, his prophetic beat poetry brought to a halt. Davie gave him some coffee shop snaps for applause.

Tripps seemed reluctant but offered Kal what he knew.

"Came on the scene a few weeks ago. Slow at first. No one was really sure where it was coming from. Got popular quick. Supply and demand, of course."

"People claimed to see the Other Side," Davie offered in the silence, his guitar off to the side.

"...false visions," Kiefer noted.

"After what sounds like a serious head trip in the bad places, dosers blacked out," Tripps concluded.

"Straight catatonic," added Davie.

"Soulless," finished Kiefer.

"Soulless?" Kal was intrigued and concerned. Demon dust stealing souls and zealous sorcerers casting the curses of forgotten death gods, this was no bad trip. This was black conjure. "Know anyone who's dosed it?"

The trio exchanged uneasy looks.

"Yeah, Reese did," says Tripps.

"Radio Reese? The dubstep guy runs with the Krank Street Krew?"

Three nodding round-rimmed sunglasses.   A chill wind rolled over the hillside.

"I want to see him."

Kal stood and the trio exchanged looks with one another.

"Can we wait to be, like, not so stoned?" asked Davie.

But Kal was already walking down the hill.

FOURTEEN

KAL KNEW THEY had crossed over onto Krank Street turf by the tags sprayed on the curb. The big K in the circle was their primary clan tag and, like tribal flags, they warned all the other gangs to steer clear or get permission to enter.   It was well past noon by the time they made the walk. Along the way, Kiefer had pointed out three eagle omens and a cloud formation that looked like the Queen of England. Davie had been strumming Stairway to Heaven as he walked and Tripps was jumping on and off of passing steps and walls.

Despite the afterglow of the buzz, Kal felt uneasy after Kiefer's prophecy. Something wasn't right in the energy of the city and the Witness Boys had confirmed his fears. He joked about a disturbance in the force but they all felt it as something very real and it only got worse when they crossed University Avenue.

The turf was a working class neighborhood in Mid-City. A few kids getting home from school, adults coming home from work or going, the sounds of traffic in every direction, little red brick houses up and down the block. Kal smelled grilled meats, fresh cut grass, car exhaust, jasmine.

"This is the place," Tripps said and they stopped. House number was 333. Kal could imagine only a few omens that could be worse.

"I'll go and get him," Kiefer offered and walked around toward the back door of the house without hesitation. Kal and the others stood at the end of the driveway and waited.

"Anyone else feel out of place?" Tripps joked.

It was true, they stood out and the community seemed to notice. Nothing threatening, just the communal acknowledgement that they were strangers here. Could also have been stoner paranoia.

Minutes later Kiefer returned leading a guy everyone in SD knew as Radio Reese. Kal remembered him spinning dub step at one of Athen's events. Charismatic life of the party type, always laughing, always having a good time. Infectious positive attitude and big pearly whites.

Not anymore.

The sickly young man Kiefer led out to the street was unsteady and slow, his gaze vacant and head empty. He moved with an extreme handicap, drooled and groaned, shuffled his feet. Reese's whole aura was dark and empty and Kal felt a sickness in his gut when he got close.

"Aw, Reese..." was all Tripps could say.

It was a tragic sight. Last week Reese was bobbing his head to some tasty jams wearing those big headphones and a grin from ear to ear. Now he was... *gone*. A walking corpse. His dark brown skin had faded to a charcoal grey and his eyes were rolled back in his head leaving only the spongy whites of blindness. He just groaned and shuffled like the walking dead.

Kal was speechless.

"This from a drug?" Davie marveled.

"He's gone," Kal murmured, circling the zombie to observe his aura and symptoms.

"Question is where'd he go?" added Kiefer.

"Trapped somewhere," Kal theorized aloud, piecing it together in his head.

He'd never actually seen it done but there was plenty of documentation on voodoo zombies. The signs were there. The lolling tongue, rolled eyes, the mindless shuffle. This wasn't a corpse in the Hollywood horror fashion, but it was certainly an empty vessel. Something or someone had taken the soul and consciousness of Radio Reese, leaving behind this wilting form.

Kal ran through a list of tests and rituals in his mind, tricks he could whip up in an attempt to locate the soul and attempt a retrieval. Maybe even learn something about this Oblivion dust.

But there was no time.

They heard the roaring engine long before catching sight of the gleaming black Escalade that screeched to a stop in the street beside them. Boots poured out onto the asphalt. All big guys with mean scowls, holding their guns skyward at the ready. Bandanas and brand jackets, each wearing an eye patch. This was the Krank Street Krew.

The boys were on their turf and no one had flagged ahead for permission to enter. Kal took a deep breath. Hostile diplomacy was normally Donnie's realm. He'd have to wing it solo.

The Krew lined up along the front of the Escalade and parted for their leader, an infamous hot head that went by the moniker Dre Daggers. He was a few inches taller than Kal and made of more brawn. Held his silver Beretta in hand and walked chest out. Kal didn't budge. Like staring down a charging gorilla you had to dig your heels in and refuse to blink.

"The fuck is this?" Dre demanded.

"Checking in on your buddy," Kal said.

"Oh right," said Dre with a leer as he leaned closer. "And who the fuck gave you permission for that?"

"What happened to him?" Kal asked.

"Who the fuck are you?"

Kal thought of a few dozen ways to cripple Dre in a word. He didn't go in for all this chest beating bullshit when bigger demons were at large. Still, he bit his tongue and maintained eye contact.

"Easy, Dre," Tripps stepped in. "No disrespect. This is the Medicine Man. Wanted to take a look at Reese to see if he could—"

"Medicine Man? I thought you looked familiar," Dre said, stepping back to get a better look at Kal. "The fuckin' witch doctor himself. Just exactly who I wanted to see."

Dre raised his silver Beretta to Kal's nose.

"Wait, Dre!"

"Stop!"

The Witness Boys were right at Kal's back and Tripps played diplomat.

"Whoa whoa, Dre, be cool man," he said, hands in the air, shades reflecting the end of the gun.

Dre glared long and hard down the barrel of his weapon at Kal's passive, unconcerned face.

"What'd you do to ma boy, freak?" Dre demanded. When Kal didn't respond, he shouted. "I said WHAT DID YOU DO TO REESE?!"

"I didn't do anything, Dre. I've been... away."

It wasn't the best defense but it was all Kal could muster in the moment. He kept his heartbeat and breathing in check. No need to panic. Not like he hadn't stared death in the face a few times already.

"Oh I know you been away, motherfucker," Dre continued. "Dropped out of the game when things got a little tough and the rest of us lost a lot o' money. You gonna pay for that."

Kal met his gaze. The words hit him good, all those guilty memories bubbling up to the surface like oiled tar. He pushed back on the sickness, willing it to behave.

"You seen the poison that did this?" Kal deflected, motioning towards Reese who was absently pawing at the fence and stumbling toward the street.

Dre gave a nod for one of his guys to help Reese to the Escalade.

"I ain't seen the black dust, no. But I saw that fucking satanic picture of the Locos," Dre said through gritted teeth and clicked back the hammer on his weapon. The boys shuffled nervously behind Kal. "That your shit?"

"I don't know what you're talking about," Kal answered honestly. He'd been tracking down information about a cursed tattoo and rumors of bad drugs but the murders hadn't reached him. "What satanic picture?"

Dre's eye twitched as he tried to read Kal's face. Deciding he must be telling the truth, the clan leader pulled out his phone and showed Kal the gruesome picture that had gone viral overnight. It was bloody, that's for sure. Severed heads on pikes and a torched corpse laid out in the goddess position. Summoning star burned into the Earth. Real deal conjure.

"Who sent this?"

"Unknown number," answered Dre. "Went out to all the clans. Somebody declared fuckin' war and if they the ones who did that to Reese, they declared it on us."

Kal looked to the trio of round sunglasses at his back. "You guys seen this?"

Tripps nodded.

Dre was quick to draw attention back to himself.

"You the only freak anyone ever saw do this kinda shit. How do I know it ain't you passin' off this poison as a trip? Sacrificing people to the devil n' shit. Huh?!"

Kal's gaze was steady. "It's not satanic. It's Aztec war magic and no, I don't roll like that."

"Who the fuck does?"

"That's what I want to know," answered Kal.

"I'll find the chemist and whoever's behind...*that*," said Kal, pointing to Dre's phone. "I think I can help Reese though, if you let me."

"Ain't no one touching Reese," Dre growled defensively. "We're takin' him up to a safe spot."

"Safe spot?"

"Safe enough," Dre said.

Kal exchanged a concerned look with Kiefer.

Dre pointed a finger at Kal's chest. "You find this sick motherfucker, you point me in his direction, got it?"

Kal saw the bloodlust in Dre's eyes. There were matching glimmers of it in all of the Krew. Reese was a cousin to Dre Daggers and part of the close-knit community to which the others belonged. They had been deeply offended and made to look foolish and were eager to strike back.

"Just be ready," was all Kal could say. He knew this would get ugly now.

"Oh, I'll be ready, Doc," Dre growled. He stepped closer, nose to nose with Kal in a menacing threat. "Somebody out there brewin' up bad medicine and you can bet your ass I'll have some blood on my knife before this is over."

The threat hung heavy in the air before the Kranks loaded Reese up in their tank of an Escalade and screeched off toward the mountains.

A long, uneasy silence followed as Kal weighed all the clues and shifting variables.

"Well that went well," Tripps joked.

Kal was silent with his troubled thoughts. He was certain now that this mysterious new clan was not only trying to flood the market with a shamanic toxins but were purposely instigating tensions between the gangs. They were stirring the trouble pot and things were heating up. Gangs were talking war.

In a fit of sparks, Meklyn returned to Kal's shoulder and in his next thought, Kal had Eden's location.

FIFTEEN

DONNIE SAT AT A burrito shop in Mission Beach watching the tourists stream by with their American flag bikinis and inflatable shark floaties. He looked rough. Felt it too. All the rules of The Game say not to smoke your own shit but Donnie had to maintain his edge to stay in business and to stay alive these days. Hell, he couldn't remember how many different pills he'd popped in the last twenty four hours. Adderall and Coke for the getup-and-go, weed to mellow out, and whiskey to stoke the fire. Not to mention his high-flying blue stars. He often wondered how far you could actually push the body before it fractured but by Donnie's figure, he wasn't all that close to the breaking point.

After an expected but still annoying half hour wait, his afternoon meeting finally decided to show. Federal Narcotics Officer Nic Gaines had been Donnie's inside contact for years. However tenuous, the partnership kept them both rich and out of jail. Gaines took one look at him and disappeared inside the souvenir shop next door. Donnie got up and followed.

The shop was a cramped little closet full of knick-knacks and useless junk. Little plastic crabs holding signs that said 'Mission Beach' and post cards with fat people that say 'Having a whale of a time in San Diego!' It was all the usual cheap tourist shit that people take back to their friends and coworkers as a way of saying 'Sorry you were stuck here while I was on vacation but, here, I brought you this reminder that I'm a world traveler.'

Donnie cozied up next to a shelf of sea shells painted various neon colors and glanced across the display case at Gaines, who looked grumpier than usual.

"Told you I don't like these open air meetings, shit brain," Gaines grumbled as he pretended to browse through the store's Chinese imports.

Gaines was a bulky guy in his forties wearing slick Ray-Ban shades and a nice suit. Did well for himself managing the local drug activity and keeping a cut of the trade. Used Federal forces to crack down on anyone who didn't want to play ball or pay the tax. Their business went way back but Gaines was still a shark in these waters and Donnie knew to tread carefully.

"Sea shell?" he offered with a grin.

"Don't fuck with me, Donnie, I'm not in the mood."

"Nic, I wouldn't have called you if it wasn't serious," Donnie said.

"Serious? You wanna talk serious, you little prick? What have you and your boy been up to lately, huh? Slinging dope wasn't enough, you gotta turn to ritual fucking sacrifice?!" Gaines took a breath to calm down and lower his voice. Donnie wondered if that vein in his forehead might rupture.

"Nic, you think Kal and I had something to do with the Locos hit?" Donnie was actually surprised. Maybe even a little flattered. "C'mon."

"Well if it ain't you then there's some other lunatic out there conjuring all that mystic magic jerk-off crap."

"Whaddya got on el Brujan?"

Gaines waved it off.

"Not much. String of unusual overdoses, brain damage, and other weird shit associated with this Oblivion compound. Guys turning into full-blown retards wandering the streets. Goddamn mess."

"It's coming from them?" Donnie was glad to get some kind of lead to go on.

"Oh yeah Oblivion is theirs. Wasn't sure about the east county mess but it adds up."

"Can I get a sample? Kal could analyze—"

Gaines is already shaking his head and eyeing a couple of bikini girls checking out at the cash register.

"DEA can't get their hands on any. Trace amounts from victims but not enough to hand off."

"What's their angle?" Donnie wondered aloud.

"Doesn't seem to be a thread linking the targets," said Gaines. "And these Brujan motherfuckers have stirred the proverbial shit pot south of the border. Heads are literally rolling far and wide as the big chiefs try to get a handle on this thing. Even these brutal gangster fuckheads are scared of the Diablo and his Brujan muscle. Some kind of

Aztec superstition or some shit, I dunno. Those boys have some sack to go and mutilate a whole east county clan, I'll tell you that."

"Something bigger's coming," Donnie said. "Don't know what it is yet but it's more than bad drugs, man."

"What do you really want?" Gaines asked, eyeing him through the display case.

"I need access to Bosley."

"Freddy Bosley? That bone knuckle fuckhead? Ha!" Gaines chuckled. "You're too late, pal."

"What do you—"

"Dead in his cell two days ago," said Gaines. "Some weird black lung thing or something. Natural causes, they think."

"Doubt it."

"He have something to do with all this?"

Donnie was already trailing off in his own thoughts. Aztec magic. Old tribal stuff. At least now he had something for Kal.

"I gotta check a lead. If you hear anything else, let me know," Donnie said absently.

"Alright but you do the same," Gaines said as he stood to leave. "Got bodies all over and brain dead junkies. Lot of heads turning to look our direction, kid. Need to pin this on someone or the Department will start sniffing around hard down here and that's bad for both of us, Donnie."

"Mostly you."

"Put a lid on this thing, DeGrassi, or I'll bury you."

Donnie took the warning in stride and turned to leave.

"Hey!" Gaines called out. "You forgetting something?"

Donnie turned and eyed him a moment. Tenuous. That was how he'd describe their partnership. He pulled a small stuffed shark from his jacket pocket and plopped it on the display case in front of Gaines. The agent gave Donnie a look of loathing over his tinted shades.

"Cute," he grumbled.

Donnie grinned and winked. They both knew it was full of money and the shark was Donnie's subtle stab at the agent's frequently ruffled feathers. Gaines slipped it casually into his pocket.

"Figure this out, kid," Gaines said. "And lay off the coke, Donnie, you look like shit."

SIXTEEN

EDEN LAY AWAKE in a cheap motel room surrounded by sea green walls and musty, matted carpet. The morning sun filtered in through thin plastic blinds and gave spotlight to the dust in the air.

The air conditioner grumbled. A fly zipped around overhead.

Eden's mind was a storm but all she could do was keep breathing.

She felt a wreck. Couldn't sleep all night. When she closed her eyes, she saw something looking at her. Leering. That thing, whatever it was, it watched her. It was always watching her. She could feel its hot breath on the back of her neck, hear the hungry grumble of its stomach. Something slimy and disgusting lurked deep in her soul and she was afraid to confront it.

Slipping into sleep was a death sentence. That's where it lived. Closing her eyes was a nightmare all in itself, so she just laid there staring at the empty wall wondering how long she could hold back her exhaustion.

"How'd you get yourself here, Edie?" she asked aloud to herself and the empty room.

The trail wound further back into the shadows of the past than she really wanted her mind to wander but it seemed so tragic. Wasn't so long ago that she couldn't wait to be free of her aunt's trailer in south Michigan. Couldn't wait to head west in search of fame and fortune and magic.

The magic she found wasn't what she expected though. Maybe it never is. You never know you're with the wrong crowd until it's too late. Unless maybe she wanted to be with the wrong crowd. To do the wrong things. To rebel and see how far it took her.

And it brought her here.

"Well played, Eden," she muttered.

Eden only came to this room because the motel owner knew her from her previous... *work*. Let her crash for free and respected her privacy. That's why she was surprised when someone knocked on the door. A streak of terror rushed through her and she sat bolt upright.

Oh God, it's him. Oh no, no, no, they found me!

These and a thousand other thoughts went to Def Con 1 in her already crowded little head.

It was agony just to pick herself up off the floral bedspread and clamber toward the window for a peek. The man she saw both shocked and relieved her. It wasn't Xechan, at least. But it was still someone who frightened her. They said he was a sorcerer too. They called him a witch doctor. They called him the Medicine Man.

Shit.

KAL SQUINTED INTO the morning sun and adjusted his aviators. Place was a dive. Couldn't believe this girl made it all the way up to Oceanside to hide out. He kept a wary eye, knowing that whoever had been toying with the dark stuff was probably looking for her and, if he and Meklyn could track her down, odds were good whoever put the curse on her had similar psychic GPS. He knocked again and peeked in the window.

"She's in there," Meklyn gurgled, hiding under Kal's jacket from the blazing sun.

"I know that, Mek," Kal sighed, leaning against the door jamb. "Can't go busting the door in."

"Sure you can," said the creature.

Kal started to knock again when the door clicked slowly open and there she stood. Wild black hair in disarray, mascara streaked down her cheeks. Stood there in ripped jeans and a half T-shirt that sported a fashion logo in the shape of a lipstick kiss.

"Hey," she murmured, squinting in the morning light, chipper as death.

"Morning," Kal said with a grin.

She didn't seem nearly as amused as he was.

AN HOUR LATER they were sitting on the roof of a nearby townhouse sipping coffee. Little place with a nice ocean view. Kal knew the owner, an investment banker who was always out of town. (Donnie wasn't the only one with connections.) Gulls screeching, waves crashing on the beach below, sea breeze smelling of salt, it was a nice change of pace for them both.

"Nice place," Eden said as she sipped awkwardly, feeling hideously out of place.

Kal had been trying to keep her calm and her mind off the obvious. Kept asking her if she surfed and if Columbian brew was alright. She was polite but a million miles away.

"Are you calm?"

"Calm?" Eden wouldn't really use that word. Ever. "I don't know, are you?"

"Sometimes," Kal admitted, rolled cigarette hanging from his mouth. "Takes practice though."

"Like meditation."

"Sorta yeah."

She was watching the sea gulls and tapping her foot. There was that big fat pink elephant on the balcony and neither of them was doing a great job of ignoring it.

"Where'd you get it?" he finally asked.

She steadied herself and motioned toward his smoke. "Can I get one of those?"

Kal handed her the cigarette without dropping his gaze. She hit it a couple times, strong pulls. The smoke wrapped around her like some slithering creature before it disappeared into the breeze.

"I done a lot of bad things in my life," she said and let that linger a moment. "But I never done anything like them."

"Who?"

"At first I thought they were just running drugs. I had that thing for bad boys with big engines and guns. Stupid I know, I just—"

She scratched her eyebrow with her thumb, trembling fingers barely holding the cigarette.

"I never expected this other shit too."

Kal watched Eden talk and handle herself, trying to sort out from the clues in her aura and body language just where she came from and how she got into this mess. It's a struggle but she's telling him how she got herself mixed up with a drug cartel dabbling in the dark arts and something about rituals but he's watching her eyes.

"Demonic shit," she concludes. "Or something."

Kal isn't surprised. That sigil tatted between her shoulder blades was something twisted and alive and nasty. Still, something bigger was going on.

"They do these... *rituals*," her voice trembled. "Robes and chanting and daggers... There's a lot of them, a big group... w-wearing masks and... there's sex and, uhm, blood and these...m-monsters..."

The cigarette dropped from her fingers and gentle sobs quaked forth streams of tears. All of it just poured out and Eden felt ashamed and embarrassed and unworthy.

Sinful...

So Disgusting...

That horrible tramp on her back with all of those---

STOP IT!

STOP!

She tried to pull it back together, sniffling and wiping her face.

Kal held his distance. Watched her energy percolate and bubble with the ripples of the Underworld. She wasn't kidding. Girl had been through some Hell and carried the residue in her soul.

"I'm sorry," she said.

"Don't be."

He stood and crossed to sit next to her, right inside the bubble where the sickness clung to him like sticky smoke.

"It's not even the stuff they did," Eden says with a hollow voice, staring far away. "It's how he seduced me into wanting it, craving it... My mind got lost in it and my body, uhm, my body *responded*. And I wanted him. He forced it. Inside I was saying *No No No* but outside was—"

Don't say it.

Outside was YES YES YES

Yes Sir, Yes Master, YES GOD!

"... but there was a wall between me and the world, I was cut off from my arms and my legs and my—"

So dirty.

"It's okay," he said.

So wrong.

"It's okay."

Broken... Disgusting... Infected...Inside me now...

"Eden, it's okay."

She looked up and realized he was right there. His eyes were icy blue, how had she not noticed that before? He was there, so intense, and whatever he was doing it silenced the thoughts that were clawing at her mind.

Her mind settled and the wind stopped and the world was still for a moment.

Kal focused and relaxed and let the sick energy drain into the Earth.

"How do you do things?" she asked. "How do you know this *other* reality?"

Kal thought for a minute, careful not to break the eye contact that was holding the psychic silence.

"Good teachers," he said.

"Like a shaman school?"

"No, not like a school."

"Then who?"

He shrugged. "Everyone."

She was persistent in the staring contest. "Everyone?"

"Turns out whether I like it or not, people find me," he said. "They need help, need to know things. They find me. People, spirits, animals. It's fuckin' weird but it's my life. They find me because whatever it is I've done or understand, even if it doesn't do much for me, it helps them. Usually."

His cosmic stare got to her. Soothed her. It was safe here. She didn't know how or why but the curse that hounded her and the powers that tormented her, in Kal's presence they were manageable. With Kal, she felt like she could win.

She broke the eye trance first. Looked down at his ink, his tattoos and markings.

Why him? Why now?

"And what helps you, Mr. Medicine Man?"

Kal thought for a minute, staring out at the setting sun, which was poised and hovering over the Pacific. It had never occurred to him before but the answer was easy.

"Being found."

Could have been a thousand suns rise and set in that moment, so outside of time and unreal. There is no good word for the true understanding two souls can have of one another in a single moment. Maybe it doesn't happen enough to name it but it happened to Eden and Kal.

And in an instant it was gone again.

Back to reality.

"Can you..." she struggles and looks away. "Can you fix it?"

Kal steadied himself. If he tried to banish that thing without knowing its pressure points like its name and symbols, he could fail and just get the thing riled up and angry. Bad for him but worse for Eden. But connecting with her there on that balcony, feeling like misfits and outsiders and kindred together, how could he say he won't even try?

"It might not work," he warned honestly. "I don't know enough about it yet. Did they tell you anything about this thing? What it was? Why they were binding it to you?"

She thought for a moment, avoiding his eyes and staring out at the drifting sea.

"All I remember is when he caught me trying to get away, they took me somewhere—I don't know where, I was blindfolded—and set up this ritual, like a pageant. When they took off the blinder, I saw people in robes and hoods. They had these masks and they were chanting something that just didn't sound... *right,* and there were candles and alien symbols and smoke."

Kal gathered the pictures from her mind as she described it. Glimpses of hoods and robes, a lame anachronism that reeked of amateurs. Someone was dabbling in something that sounded cooler than it really was. He had to hand it to them though. These guys knew the basics.

The circle of figures forms the coven, a linkage of minds that co-create a shared reality. The leader was wearing a similar robe but a blood red color with a golden rope tied around his waist. He held an ornate dagger that seemed important to the puzzle, some sort of clue to the power of whatever was about to be summoned into Eden.

The images Kal was getting were disturbing. He heard animal noises from somewhere, maybe a sacrifice. Screams. Blood. Skull faces all circled together. Hoods were lowered and the coven were wearing bone masks of death, some of them with animal masks and helmets. A circle of jackal and skull headed acolytes.

"The whole thing started to blur. I don't know if it was just fear or the stuff they were burning but I felt a little funny and then started to lose focus and... I think I passed out."

Her voice hung in the air as Kal continued to watch the flickering images in her aura, those repressed and haunted memories from her subconscious. These things float around a person all the time if you activate the Sight. Eden leaked glimpses of some horrible torture, some invasion of darkness, and the tattoo that inked itself into her flesh from the inside, the entity's abstract and symbolic name claiming her body as its vessel.

This kind of thing was sort of a legend in occult circles, a fantasy of crazed megalomaniacs, but to actually do it... to actually perform such a twisted blasphemy...

"I... I'm sorry," was all Kal could mutter.

He covered her with a blanket and sat quietly next to her for a few minutes as the images went dark and there was just the breeze and the screeching gulls, both of them trembling in the mutual silence.

This thing had to go.

He stood from the bench and walked back toward the condo.

"We'll get this thing," he promised on the way. "Tonight."

Kal walked back into the condo, pulling his Android from his pocket. As the phone rang on the other end, he ran through a list of things he'd need. He didn't know the entity's name. All he had was the symbol and something to do with a dagger.

"Yeah go," Donnie answered.

"Get over here, fucker," Kal said. "And I need you to pick up some supplies."

"Say what?"

Kal stared out at the dark haired girl beneath the blanket.

"Calling in a full blown exorcism."

SEVENTEEN

THE CREATURE THAT looked back from the mirror was a nightmare to behold. Sculpted flesh wrapped in tattoos and scars gave it the look of a demon but it was the eyes that made it terrible. It was the bloodlust in those black animal orbs, something murderous with the burning rage of a zealot.

An intense, unblinking stare in awe and reverence was all the beast offered in response to what he had become. His body was lean, his skin like a canvas full of writhing black adornments placed reverently in ink and woven with scars. A testament to his faith, temple to the dark god. The man had become a symbol and, by his own measure, touched immortality.

Xechan smiled at his reflection, that gruesome visage, and a flush of excitement ran through his muscles. Tattooed and scarred, he had stepped forward from obscurity to become the archon of the age. The messenger of the gods. One of the hooded attendants draped a ceremonial black jaguar pelt over his broad shoulders and Xechan ground his teeth in anticipation.

"*Belloch Mictlan,*" he murmured in prayer.

DONNIE PARKED ON a street lined with identical little beach townhouses and grabbed a paper bag full of supplies from his backseat. He'd lived in SoCal for more than ten years now and its odd diversity never ceased to amaze. Earlier this morning he was investigating a killer drug in a run-down ghetto east of downtown and now he stood surrounded by the summer houses of the rich, ready to help his buddy exorcise a demon from some girl he'd met off the street.

Just another day in the life.

"You get everything?" Kal demanded eagerly as he opened the door for Donnie.

"I need a drink first."

Donnie plowed on into the kitchen where pieces of the ritual were collecting across the countertops.

The lights were dimmed to allow the hallowed orange glow of candles to bring shadows to the many corners of the condo. A flat screen at least six feet wide hung on the wall playing cartoons on mute while some dark industrial trance beats growled out of hidden speakers around the room. Kal had a smattering of tools scattered across the counter tops; knives, table salt, multi-colored pills, a voodoo doll made of paper towels and twist ties, and a copy of People magazine with all the eyes blacked out.

Donnie did his best to ignore the accoutrement as he slid a bottle of Jim Beam from its brown paper sleeve. Poured himself a strong drink as he looked around at the local digs. Sleek, modern stainless steel in the kitchen, vintage red brick, and the open loft feel with furniture out of the catalogs.

"You moved up in the world," he said, knocking back a beastly gulp from the tumbler.

"Yeah," Kal muttered absently. He paced around the room wiggling his fingers and twitching one eye.

The place was nice, but that's not why Kal liked it. It happened to sit on a cross section of ley lines that ran up and down the Pacific coast. Pathways of subtle energies in the Earth gathered here in a potent little knot that made for a perfectly balanced ritual space. He was feeling them out as he wandered around the room like some mad hobo, spinning in circles with his palms out, murmuring strange incantations with erratic breathing patterns, and looking for just the right place to draw up the circle.

The supplies Kal had requested included tobacco, garlic, red wine, a brass compass, several cans of spray paint, and a serrated knife with a carved skull handle. Most important, the six pack of Monster energy drinks came out of the bag last. Kal liked to load up on super-caffeine before an exorcism because, so he claimed, the increased adrenaline helped to solidify his mental shields. Plus the cans all read "unleash the beast" with a claw mark that looked suspiciously like three Arabic sixes. Anything to set the mood. Kal's rituals were about tweaking the reality perceived by the minds present. Especially his own.

"You gonna tell me what this is all about?" Donnie finally asked. "Can't say I'm not preoccupied at the moment."

"This isn't your arena, I know, but I need a second mind," Kal said.

"Who's this girl? Cute?"

"Possessed."

"You have a way of attracting the freaks."

A creaking door drew their attention and Eden stepped quietly from the bathroom. Freshly showered, she wore a plush white bathrobe she found in the hall closet and worked a brush through her tangled locks of dark hair. The lack of makeup and grime made the gentle curve of her face and the subtlety of her complexion more visible. She had an Eastern European look with soft eyes and smooth pale skin. A full minute passed before either man blinked but it was Donnie who finally gathered his wits.

"Hi there," he said, extending a hand. "Donnie DeGrassi."

"Eden," she said quietly, ignoring the hand.

It didn't take long for Eden to gather that Donnie was a man of several conflicting thoughts and crossed to the couch to try and block them out before they made her blush. She took her seat, eyes on the floor as she waited for Kal to find a spot near the fireplace that seemed to have the right mojo. He tasted the air and placed a hand on the floorboards to gauge the tilt of subtle forces.

"Here."

Kal grabbed a jar from the counter and poured a thin circle of salt in a wide circle around him. Donnie watched with a cocked eyebrow and poured himself another drink.

A PAIR OF MILITARY grade boots, jet black and laced tightly, paced a hypnotic cadence around the perimeter of a poorly illuminated barn hidden deep in the middle of nowhere.

CLYP. CLYP. CLYP.

The pace was intentional. The tight clicks of his heels on the barn's concrete floor outlined a structured, methodical trance on behalf of the assembled coven. There were exactly twelve of them, each robed in traditional black and crowned with masks favoring the bone face of death. They were a regiment of expertly trained soldiers and ritual sorcerers whose sole glory was to serve the Avatar of Darkness, the archon they called Xechan.

In his stead, the men answered to a lieutenant they called Bael.

Without words he corrected one or two soldiers on their stance. A good swift swat on the arm or leg with his leather riding crop was all it took to get them standing at proper attention. A grin worked its way across his face when he turned and saw through his signature red lenses the assembled legion. His occult army. Assassins of the highest caliber. All his work and planning finally coming together.

Then they heard Him enter.

Upon Xechan's arrival to their unholy sanctuary the entire coven dropped to a knee in reverence for their leader. Bael bowed his head but remained standing. Xechan paid zero regard to any of them, his eyes were firmly focused on the towering effigy they had erected overhead. It was fastened to the wall of the barn and rose up to wrap onto the ceiling, a hideous likeness of their patron deity with arms stretched out over the world.

"Belloch Mictlan," said Xechan.

"Belloch Mictlan!"

The chorus of twelve voices sent Xechan's mind and energy racing into the abyss as he walked through the circle. Torches cast dancing shadows up the walls and the bony corpse god looked down on him with empty eye sockets.

Mictlantecuhtle, the God of Death, Pestilence, and Suffering. And the Aztec Lord of Dark Magic.

"Belloch Mictlan!"

At the base of the effigy was the altar, just behind Bael, where two red chalices sat on either side of the idol, full to the brim with pure gasoline.   Bound and gagged at the base of the altar were five squirming bodies.   That's all they were too. Bodies.   These were the zombie victims of Oblivion, the soulless walkers presented to their dark god for his consumption.

Xechan turned to his cultists and repeated their mantra. "Belloch Mictlan!"

The priests rose to their feet, each wearing the bony skeletal face of their clan, and echoed his call.

"Belloch Mictlan!"

DONNIE LEANED AGAINST the island counter and watched his best friend dance (literally, he was dancing) the line between lunatic and dark genius. The lights were all off now, save the radiant black lights that cast glowing purple auras into the shadows of the room alongside candles and the big screen playing an old Looney Toons episode. The grunge trance music, the incense, and then there was the paint. Kal had splattered and sprayed cans of red and yellow along the walls, ceiling, and floor in a disastrous mess reminiscent of an unsupervised preschool. It was glow paint too so the whole effect was neon madness.

After getting a finger-painted zodiac symbol just right on the brick fireplace mantle, Kal joined Donnie at the kitchen counter and cracked open one of the tall black cans of liquid energy.

"You were telling me about this cartel that's into conjure, right?" Kal said in between gulps. Donnie nodded, content with his tumbler of whiskey. "I'm pretty sure she's carrying around one of their curses."

Donnie paused and regarded the shy girl in the bath robe. "You're serious?"

Kal finished off the first energy drink and crushed the can, shaking his head at the sudden rush and belching loudly. "Yeah. Something's been linked to her. A, uh, an *entity*. We gotta get it out."

He cracked a second can and continued gulping.

"You're saying El Brujan cursed her with a demon?" Donnie mused, watching Eden.

"Or something."

At the mention of the cartel, she looked up.

"You know them?" Eden asked.

"I'm starting to," Donnie said. "What can you tell me about—?"

"Not now," interrupted Kal, the brain freeze contorting his face as he crushed the second can. "Their leader is a sorcerer calls himself Xechan. Thinks he's a badass when it comes to conjure. He could have a link to her through that nasty squiggle, we gotta get it out. Okay, Eden, in the circle you go."

Kal was already buzzing with the energy fizz, speaking rapidly and twitching around the room. He led Eden to the circle and she laid face down in the middle, the robe draped over her to conceal the tattoo in question. Kal's gentle hand on her back reassured her that everything was going to be alright and she closed her eyes to ready her mind as they had practiced.

"Donnie, I need you to hold a circle," Kal said. "Just like before."

"I heart hypnosis," DeGrassi mumbled sarcastically and plopped down into a chair.

"Right," Kal said, busying himself with placing tools and ritual paraphernalia around the circle. "I need you to count yourself into a deep trance and draw a psychic circle around the room. You gotta hold that trance barrier, Donnie, no matter what you hear around you. Can I trust you with this?"

Donnie had let Kal get him into some strange shit, stuff that would make anyone uncomfortable, but an exorcism was new on the list. He sighed and shook his head. He'd lived through it all so far.

"Guess so," he muttered.

"No guess work, brother, this is dangerous," Kal insisted, his eyes already getting that crazy look to them.

Donnie locked eyes with Kal. "I got it. Let's do this so I can ask some more questions."

"Okay."

THE CHANTING WAS an unintelligible droning accompanied by the war drum stomps of the twelve Brujan acolytes. It filled Xechan's head and aided the settling of his otherworldly trance. Kneeling before the effigy of Mictlantecuhtle, smoke in the air and a haunted chill across his bare skin, Xechan opened his mind and soul to the under realm.

A pair of priests circled him with red chalices, flicking gasoline onto his flesh like holy water.

Visions played in his mind.

Visions of long hallways and death. Shrouded faces and the burning away of the world.

He murmured his prayers to Mictlan and removed the black pelt revealing a beast-like form splayed out before the altar. Xechan had been through all the initiations, passed through all the levels of the brujo. In his mind, he was the archon of the Aeon, the messenger of the Old Gods. He had a mission, charged by the death god to bring a warning to the world. To open the gate.

But first he had to finish his devotional work, completing the human artwork he had crafted of himself. Xechan knelt down before the idol and presented the canvas of his flesh to his lieutenant.

Bael's cold eyes fell on the single piece of unadorned skin in the middle of the cult leader's back. The last piece of the puzzle was all that remained to complete the artwork that would summon a new world. He allowed himself a delicious grin and prepared his tools—needle, chisel, dagger—with reverence and a certain anxious anticipation. The gathered acolytes offered their chanting and prayers, whipping up a disturbing vibration in the space.

"The bonds of this reality are loosening," said Bael as he worked the needle and ink into his king's flesh. "The darkness is getting closer."

The piercing of the needle was a sweet release for el diablo, a source of twisted pleasure. The sharp jabs into his flesh brought him closer to the threshold of the Other Side. The pain was a catalyst for the dark consciousness. And he relished it.

KAL TOOK A DEEP breath and summoned his invisible ally.

Meklyn, put up a shield and be ready to knock me out if it gets loose.

It was bad enough this little beastie was shacked up in Eden's soul. If it got any further into his own subconscious, it would have access to all of Kal's knowledge and memories and might become a bigger nuisance.

Meklyn was pretty territorial of Kal's mind, especially after the last little incident with this particular tattoo. If anything tried to get in that neither of them wanted, the imp would just knock him out and slam the door shut. As for Eden, that would be up to Kal.

He steadied himself over Eden's body as Donnie counted himself down into a deep trance in the chair by the window. Kal's heart was already racing with all the added caffeine and temporary energy but he stilled his mind to a controlled whisper. He could sense the psychic shield Donnie was knitting around the condo from his deep trance and Kal breathed his own energy and power into it.

He summoned the protection seal of Solomon to the front of his mind, backed up with half a dozen elemental wards and the paw print of his own power animal for good strong measure. Glowing neon sigils blazed around him in his peripheral. A few sprinkled herbs, some words spoken to the Greater Beings, couple protector spirits invoked, and Meklyn's fire shield blazing in the ether around them; Kal was ready.

135

He took a breath, glanced at Donnie, and slipped the bath robe down below the ink on Eden's back and braced himself for the sigil.

Searing!   *Evil!*   *Pain like*

Suffering like   Tor--   ment...

That pummeling again, that violence against his own strained brain matter! Soul torture...

He willed a concentrated focus, held forward the image of Solomon's Seal, and like staring into an oncoming rush of direct energy, the mental attacks from the sigil skipped and grazed off to the sides around him. A storm of noise filled his head, the blazing chords of death metal and a howling from the volcanic core of the Earth. He stared into the onrushing tunnel, down into the depths of the demon's hiding place, somewhere inside Eden's mind and she winced in pain. He placed his hands on her shoulders to steady her and analyzed the glyph.

It was a jagged pile of connected angles overlapping an inverted pentagram and woven with ancient astrological symbols. Had to be Babylonian.

No. Aztec...

He felt the thing inside notice his presence, saw eyes open beneath the inked stars on either side of the girl's spine, and something woke up in the dark...

SOMEWHERE FAR AWAY a low rumble shook the room, or maybe just his bones. It rattled him from head to toe until Xechan was suddenly screaming, suspended alone over an open pit that yawned into unfathomable darkness below the world.

The pit breathed against him and the foul odor of the under realm worked its way into his nose and guts, and he held back the urge to be sick.

...with every needle jab the visions came...

He was alone in the dark.   Alone at the feet of an ancient and primordial entity.

The tattoos moved and writhed on his skin like living snakes...

That vision, like before, filled Xechan's mind as he hung naked and vulnerable above the limitless abyss.   That vision of blood and bullets.

A sidewalk along a five way intersection in a town called Culpas, Mexico.

A young boy buying an ice cream.

Pain wracked his body and the visions skipped ahead. Cars from all directions, men with angry war cries and a spray of ammunition that bit into the crowd like hell's hornets.

The world slowed and the shadows crept up from below as bodies exploded in red showers around him, the young boy's first glimpse at the bloody war of drugs and money on the streets of his home. The raging violence. The insane mob. The bullets like rain overhead and all around, cutting down soldiers and civilians alike.   A blood bath. A shower.

And somehow I survived.

Somehow.

The god leaning over him breathed putrid, frigid air onto the boy's neck and goose bumps coated his tattoos.

That boy died. The one who came out of that unholy baptism was a man with a vision.

A man with a name.

Xechan.

SOMETHING PUSHED OUT, rushed forward through the ether, punched Kal square in the frontal lobe of his brain and he staggered back. The blow was hard but he forced himself not to look away before he closed what he'd just opened.

Meklyn...

The beast inside of Eden rose up through the ink, slithered its way off of her skin in a hissing, alien cloud to stare Kal in the face. It was like slithery smoke, a trick of the light, but it was alive and aware. The thing leaned toward Kal, showing him a movie projected on the back of his mind, a horror film of death and destruction and terror...

"Meklyn!"

It was laughing at him. At his foolishness and Kal felt small before it. Puny. Weak. A writhing shadow, an ink-made serpent, it was a tyrant among hellspawn and it looked deep into his insecurities and folded itself in on his fear.

And then it communicated something in a voice that rang out like microphone feedback in the inner ear...

"When you stare into the abyss... The abyss stares back into you..."

The voice echoed around the room and Donnie's attention wavered, the psychic shell around the house flickering as a result.

THE NEEDLE AND CHISEL drove Xechan further into trance where he saw the long hall of Mictlan. The bony face of his idolatrous deity. Mictlantecuhtli leaned forward and breathed ice cold *unlife* into his champion.

Mictlan will come here to lead the charge of Armageddon—

to wipe out this corrupted life to bones and dust

so the new world can be born.

The earth revolving around the sun.

The animals have despoiled the world in their greed and hubris.

Conquered the biosphere and destroyed life and the balance,

...once again...

The animal race must be purged and cleansed to bring back balance.

The sixth sun dawns only when the darkness of death's realm has purged the earth of evil.

As the visions swarmed him like spirits and wracked his mind with overload, Xechan's soul exploded in revelation and he felt the embodiment of his god—FINALLY!—that terrifying and exhilarating experience. That terrible dark communion.

Blood pumping battery acid, skin crawling alive, stomach churning, tattoos and scars raking across him in dancing movements over his skin, his entire body bleeding through the pores.

The man was horrified but the uplifting fervor of his faith carried him to a higher place.

It is not punishment, it is praise. It is a gift.

Apotheosis.

Xechan was not here by accident. He did not shrink away from the presence of the dark one.

And he was rewarded.

It was like a poison raging through him. Blessing and purifying him. Making him the Archon.

The bringer of destruction. The ambassador of the Gods, delivering the Earth to the feet of the Queen of Chaos. Kali dances her many arms and bares her teeth.

He hovered there above the abyss that lay open beneath the barn, a vast uncaring pit of emptiness, trembling even as he heard the monstrous yawn echo across the silence and rattle his bones.

He felt the kiss of death.

The Queen has such eyes . . .

"Find my vessel so I may be with you there, might consume and satisfy you."

Xechan's eyes burst to awareness and in that moment he knew where to find his lost Eden.

KAL WAS ELBOWED HARD in the nose, blood splattering across his face as he fell back against the couch. Eden leapt to her feet and whirled around to bare down on him. Her eyes were black and bleeding and her teeth were fangs and she hissed like some snake had taken possession of her.

"Eden!"

Things had gotten out of control. Without time to think, Kal kicked her legs out and forced his right palm in her face, showing the All Seeing Eye to the heinous evil taking hold of her from within. The entity screeched and recoiled. Eden stumbled and Kal lurched to catch her, pinning her to the floor.

Meklyn strengthened the fire shield around them and, drawing on its power, Kal pushed against the girl's mind, forcing the entity into a corner long enough to get a grip on her lower neck where the pressure point was located.

He got his thumb in position just as the demon's power came surging back up to belch corrosive acid into the air. It splashed his forearm and burned like hell but Kal held the pressure point a few more seconds.

"Stare, Junkie, Stare into that abyss!" a voice not wholly Eden's screeched aloud before finally she lost consciousness in his arms. He slopped his free hand through the red paint on the floor and pressed a red hand print into her back, covering the cursed tattoo with a seal.

The dark aura of the room faded as though the power cord had been pulled and a stunning hush fell over them all. Kal leaped to his feet to turn on lights and blow out candles, banishing the ritual as far away as he could.

You see him?

"I saw him."

Meklyn knew as well as Kal that the man they had seen across the astral was the *diablo of el Brujan*. He had been there. Watching.

Kal snapped firmly at Donnie's ear and he woke suddenly from his trance.

A moment passed as they gathered their thoughts.

The white light was harsh and the room was full of the burning smell of snuffed candles.

"How'd it go?" Donnie asked.

Kal just looked at him, wild-haired, drained, and splattered in blood red paint.

"I saw him."

Donnie set his jaw. "What's he want?"

"Her," Kal answered with a gesture toward Eden, unconscious on the floor. She laid there quite still, breathing softly. "She's the key to Armageddon."

"Lucky her."

"Lucky us."

EIGHTEEN

WHEN THAT BLOOD RED ball of fire gets swallowed up by the vast, uncaring ocean at the end of the day, it's like the whole world just lost its light and now the night comes back to power. Kal and Donnie sat exhausted and beat up on the balcony, enjoying the night air and having a smoke.

"You ever think about getting away from all this?" Donnie asked absently.

"What you think I've been trying to do the past few months?"

"Yeah but you're still here," Donnie said. "I mean go somewhere like Fiji or Indonesia, far away where no one knows you and this whole fucked up world is a million miles away."

"Can't outrun my world," Kal said ominously. "Finally burned out, are you?"

Donnie kept his eyes on the dark ocean and just shrugged.

Kal thought for a minute, pulling another drag off his hand-rolled smoke.

"It's all connected but I can't figure how just yet. The demon, the zombie drugs, El Brujan. It's all ...big. Something's coming, Donnie. Just around the bend in time. I can't see enough of the shape just yet to figure what it is."

"Guess we keep investigating then," Donnie said, stabbing out his cigarette and tossing it over the rail.

"Rather let someone else handle it," Kal sighed.

"You know better than that, buddy. The only assholes capable of dancin' with death... are us."

Eden stepped to the doorway and her presence interrupted them. Kal stood to meet her.

"How you feeling?" he asked.

She gave him a nod, dressed now and tucked up in a blanket. Her face was tired and worn but some of the burden had lifted. Looked like she finally got some sleep but could use ten times more.

Donnie's phone rang with a rock 'n roll tune. Kal and Eden didn't seem to notice.

"Am I... I mean is it...?" Eden stuttered awkwardly in a whisper.

Kal stepped all the way to her. He wanted to tell her it was all over but that would be a lie and they both knew it.

"It's bandaged for now," he said and that was good enough.

"Kal," said Donnie with a serious tone. "We got something. Group of kids in La Jolla dosed Oblivion."

That was all he needed to hear.

DONNIE PULLED THE CAR to a screeching halt at the curb and the trio piled out. Above them rose the bleached walls of a La Jolla mansion, the kind that looked like it was designed for architectural magazines rather than people's actual lives. Trash and red Solo cups were strewn across the immaculate front lawn alongside a couple of passed out teenagers. All the lights were burning inside but the place was eerily quiet.

Donnie led his rescue crew right in the front door where a cluster of adolescents huddled in a nervous pack in the den to the left. One of them caught sight of Donnie and leaped forward.

"Donnie, I'm so sorry, man, so sorry," he stammered.

"Easy, buddy," Donnie said to calm him down.

Jose was a good kid. Dumb as rocks but good. Didn't bother to breathe as he fell over himself explaining what happened.

"He's out man, he's—Oh god, I think he's dead. I think he's— *Oh Jesus*," the kid ran his hands through his hair and trembled. "It's Olin, man. I think he—"

"Clear out," Kal ordered, getting his mind straight to business.

Donnie waved the group along and they dispersed into various open rooms of the house and into the night. The parting crowd revealed the victim splayed out on the living room carpet. Seventeen year old kid with a solid build, football player type. Body was twitching and spasming, eyes rolled back in his head, mocha brown skin turning a sickly green.

The kid coughed and gurgled, sending a pair of girls into panicked shrieks. Eden put her arms around one and offered her comfort to calm them.

Kal studied the victim closely. "Tell me exactly what happened."

"I don't know, it's Olin, man," Jose stammered. "He brought it with him, something new he wanted to dose."

"Where'd he get it?" Kal demanded.

He was propping up Olin's head with a pillow and checking vital signs. Listened to his chest for heart and breathing rhythm, took his pulse on the left wrist, checked his eyes which were rolled back into his skull, and swiped his finger over Olin's forehead to taste the sweat. Whole time he was peering into the kid's aura, the field looking dark and toxic, a mud hole of dead energy. Bad juju clung to him like disease.

"Probably his regular guy, I don't know," Jose answered. Poor kid was sweating, nervous. No doubt the lot of them were terrified with concern for their friend and the prospect of bringing on trouble.

"It's this," said a tall, skinny girl who handed Kal a little black plastic baggie. Kal shook the remaining contents out into his hand. Tiny dab of grey powder that smelled like grave moss and blood. First whiff brought to Kal's mind images of bones shifting through earth and egg sack pods of some amphibious critter. His stomach churned with horrible possibilities.

"This happen right away?" Kal asked. He was still checking over the victim's vitals and prodding the astral space around his head. There was no sign of consciousness in there. The body was deteriorating but the driver wasn't even behind the wheel.

"Uh, yeah," Jose stammered, trying to remember. "He snorted it and went like *WHAM* over backward, like something hit him and knocked him on his ass. We laughed and thought, you know, it was a good trip or whatever. I was gonna hit it next but then... then he started freaking out."

"Body was like spazzing out and shit, he started screaming like some nightmare shit was happening—" chimed in another spectator in the crowd.

"...and then he just... went quiet. Like this," Jose finished.

"Damn," Kal muttered.

Donnie leaned down close to Kal and gave the victim a once-over.

"What is it?" he asked.

"Definitely the bad medicine," Kal said, mind racing. "We need a clear, safe ritual space. I need to retrieve his soul if I still can."

A hush fell over the crowd.

Jose choked out, "Is that a joke?"

"Come on, let's get him to the dining room table," Kal urged and Donnie didn't hesitate. He helped Kal hoist Olin's unconscious body off the floor and they side-stepped across the room.

That's when Meklyn shrieked and landed on Kal's shoulder, invisible to everyone else.

"Not now, Meklyn!" Kal shouted, confusing the crowd of kids around him.

"Soldiers in black around the corner," the imp gurgled. "Sorcerers of the black blood."

Kal stopped in his tracks, nearly dropping Olin's shoulders. "Come again."

Meklyn clarified, "El Brujan. With guns. Two minutes!"

"Shit. We have to go," Kal said.

"You mean leave?" Donnie asked.

"Go. We have to move, go!" and they were moving for the door.

"Eden, stay close."

"What's happening?" she asked, following them out the door and across the front lawn.

"They're coming for you," Kal said ominously.

Eden turned white as a sheet and bolted for the car, pulling open the doors and flipping the seat forward.

Donnie told Jose to call the cops and get everyone home safe. "And, for god sake, don't ever dose something new without checking with me, you got it?"

Jose nodded and broke for the house, phone in hand. They got to the car just as two black SUVs roared around the corner, tires screeching and flames bursting from exhaust pipes.

"Shit shit go!" Kal shouted, shoving Olin's body into the backseat.

Eden dove into the back and the guys piled in. Donnie flicked the gear stick and stomped on the gas and the Jag went screeching into the night as gunfire exploded behind them.

Donnie took the curved drive downhill at top speed, tires sliding and smoking.

Bullets cracked the tinted glass of Donnie's car and Eden shrieked in surprise.

"Shit! Shit!" was all any of them could manage. "There!"

Donnie whipped the Jag onto Nautilus Avenue and sped across several lanes of traffic causing horns to blare in a shrill chorus as the Brujan trucks gave chase.

"Whaddya got for me, buddy?" Donnie asked, eyes peeled studiously on the road, occasionally flicking up to the rear view mirror to check on their pursuers.

Kal tried to gather his wits. Mind reeling, he couldn't help but wonder how his simple little life of exile on the beach had come to this in just a couple days.

"Second," he said and forced his mind to a quiet.

Quiet... How did I get here...

High speed chase through the hills and valleys of San Diego, a roaring caravan of Mexican sorcerer soldiers firing at them from behind. In the back seat was Eden, a girl from the streets possessed by a nasty spirit, and next to her lay a teenage kid who had fallen victim to a drug called Oblivion that turned him into a living zombie whose soul was somewhere in the underworld, eyes rolled back in his head and tongue lolling around.

Kal breathed it all away, tried to focus, but all he could hear was a mess of white noise. Psychic attacks were being hurled from the cars behind them, causing static in Kal's head that made it hard to think at all. A head trip in high speed.

Donnie was doing his best but he too felt the strange blanket fall over his thinking faculties. He swerved violently to correct a wobbling course.

"What's wrong?" Eden asked.

"Something in my head," he said.

He was getting dizzy and distracted. Someone was hexing him.

"Shit shit shit!" was all Donnie could sputter as he worked the wheel back and forth.

The chase was a nutty race across sanity. Donnie's driving was no stunt special but he managed to peel and squeal across the highway, under the downtown overpass, down several side streets, and along a cliff's edge before Kal came out of his trance.

"Turn right," was his sudden instruction and Donnie whipped the Jag into a drift.

Kal ordered Meklyn into the air to distract their attackers. The imp shot into the sky, a translucent red spirit streaking through the night. Kal used his familiar's eyes to survey the scene from above. The cartel trucks were gaining on the Jag and bullets were still spraying across the road. Kal wasn't the only conjurer in this fight. He knew the Brujan soldiers had a psychic edge that needed blunted.

Blast 'em, he ordered and Meklyn dove on the black SUVs.

He swooped overhead and dropped psychic fire across their windshields, an invisible wall of thought junk to cloud the sorcerers' vision. The static cleared in Donnie's mind and Kal focused his energy through Meklyn, sending the pet diving again toward the racing vehicles.

Their combined focus landed on the front right tire of the first SUV and with just a little concentrated energy—

BAM!

It exploded, jerking the truck to the side just in time to smash through the guard rail and tumble off the cliff into the ocean waves below.

"One down," Kal murmured, mostly for Meklyn. The creature was circling back around for another run, tickled to giggles with the mayhem unraveling in its wake.

"One to go," the creature retorted and swooped in for the second car.

These were occultists in the pursuing car and powerful in their own right. One of them squinted through his mask to see the spectral creature shooting through the night sky. The Brujan Priest had been well trained by his masters and had no trouble tapping into the Dark Current to funnel chaotic energy through his malice-ridden thoughts. A concentrated beam of psychic energy rippled through the sky and blasted Meklyn mid-flight. The blast hit like a rifle and scorched the imp to charred hellfire, enveloping him in a void of mixed frequencies and zapping him out of existence.

Like that, the imp was gone.

"AYYGH!!"

The attack sent Kal into a fit of screaming agony as a piece of his psyche was ripped off like a frail appendage.

"What is it?" Eden shouted.

Kal couldn't say it, couldn't form the thought.

Meklyn?!

He didn't want to believe it was possible.

"Mek!"

This had gone too far. He was two steps behind the Brujan now and that was no way to play ball. Too many lives were at stake.

They needed someplace safe.

Kal was dizzy and losing focus now, handicapped by the loss of his familiar.

"Where do I go, Kal?" Donnie bellowed, still focused on driving eighty miles per hour down residential streets.

Through the pain in his skull, the dull tearing of a slice to the frontal lobe, all Kal could think and manage to say was, "Mab's. We have to get to Mab's."

NINETEEN

THERE'S A MARKETPLACE in Chula Vista that few ever notice. A place that only exists if you know where to look. A place where sorcery can be bought and omens received. At night the place is quiet and primed with an expectant energy lurking in every shadow.

Eden nearly shook as she crept through the dark alley that wound around behind the little brick storefronts, her stomach twisted in knots. Everywhere she looked there were little black skulls with half-burned candles on their heads and twisted little voodoo dolls hanging from lamp posts. Black cats slinked around in the shadows and bats darted through the pools of light.

The lane ended at a creepy little herb shop with faint painted letters that read $A POTHECARY$. An orange neon sign in the shape of an open palm illuminated the long shadows down the alley.

"Red door," Kal directed as Donnie led the way.

Kal was doing his best to hold it together as he and Donnie carried the unconscious overdose victim through the night. His mind still burned from the trauma of losing Meklyn and his body was starting to ache from wrestling the howler attached to Eden. Worse was his impending anxiety over coming face to face with the only family he'd ever known, a woman he hadn't dared to face in years.

They made it to the back door of the shop and Kal drew a steadying breath. Donnie reached for the gnarled brass knocker to give it a couple of raps. He didn't have to. Before his hand could make contact with the portal it jerked inward revealing a stout smoking dragon of a woman looking up at them with a surly scowl.

Her sudden presence startled Donnie and Eden.

"Oh, wow…"

"Hi…"

Kal had trouble meeting her gaze but she remained silent and motionless until he did.

"I didn't know where else to go," he said, leaning against the cold brick.

"Ain't no place else," replied Mab in a voice scratched from years of smoking.

She let the door creak further open and disappeared inside.

That was about as much of an invitation as Kal was likely to get so he took it. Ushered his friends inside, gave a final glance up the lane, and closed the door behind him.

It was warm in the back room of Mab's shop, a place as antique as it was cozy. Old hand-carved furniture and throw pillows crowded the perimeter along with gaudy lamps draped in various warm fabrics like the parlor of some old time gypsy.

"Right here," Kal grunted.

The boys cleared the table in the middle of the room and laid Olin's unconscious body on top. Relieved of the burden, it was all Kal could do to make it to a nearby chair before collapsing into a coughing fit. He needed the Joos but didn't dare tell Mab.

Mab stood like a wraith in the shadows of the space and watched him with steel eyes as she pulled a Black & Mild cigarillo from a case on the shelf and lit it with a zippo. A woman of some age and a dignified poise, Mab was stout with chocolate skin some mix of Creole and South American. She wore a floral patterned moo moo and her hair was done up in a rather elaborate beehive. Skull necklaces adorned her chest in layers, jewelry of bone sticking out of her hair and ears. Her eyes flared orange in the dark behind her burning cigarillo and she smoldered looking down on Kal.

"Hiya, Mab," Kal grunted, wiping his mouth and shaking off the fit.

"Bout time you come 'round," she said in that voice like dusty gravel. "I see ye done well for ye'self."

Kal slumped a moment, the weight of a long overdue conversation heavy on the room.

"Not now," he said. "That boy needs help."

"Looks to me as all y'all need help."

Kal stood and crossed to the table where the teenage victim was splayed out, eyes rolled back in his head, limbs jerking sporadically. His skin had lost more of its pigment and he was beginning to look like a grey corpse.

"I got a lot to answer for," Kal said. "But there's some bad mojo laid on this boy. Needs a soul retrieval. I know I don't deserve your help, Mab, but he ain't done nothin' wrong except be young and stupid."

Donnie watched with great interest as Kal humbled himself before this fearsome woman. He had only met her once himself and in passing, back when they were just getting started in the Game.

Kal had been running with gangsters and insulting the Gods, Mab had told him in disgrace last they met. The rift hadn't been repaired since. All Donnie knew, now confirmed by her very presence, was that she was one of the most feared and respected medicine women around. Taught Kal a lot and brought him up when he had no one else.

Mab cast an eye to Donnie suddenly as though catching a whiff of his thoughts and his eyes darted instinctively to the floor. She surveyed Eden too, the poor girl completely unsure how to act or what to say and, as it was clear that Mab saw right through her in a second, she kept herself small and quiet in the corner, trying to keep her nervous fidgeting under control.

"You brought a lot of bad juju to my doorstep, Kalvin Renley," she said with the strong authority of a scolding grandmother. Kal nodded, chin up and answering for his deeds.

Mab seemed to have more to say but she turned her attention to the boy on the table. Placed a hand on his forehead and walked a wide circle scanning his aura.

"He doesn't have much time," she said. "Cold cloth from the closet."

Donnie turned to follow orders. Relieved to have the help, Kal returned his focus to the boy.

"Substance was snorted," he said, pulling the baggie from his pocket and tossing it on the table. "Necromantic pigment. Something unfamiliar."

Mab examined it suspiciously. "Red brick dust in a circle. Black candle. Fossil bone."

As she called out tools and ingredients, Kal and Donnie worked their way across the cluttered shelves and around the room's bizarre curios to seek them out. Mab's combined shop and home was crowded with shelves of various chemicals and powders, potions in little glass vials, old bones, and trinkets made from twisted wire and stone. It resembled a museum of occult artifacts and strange magic.

The ritual space they assembled in the middle of the room began to look like a Native American drama performed by a passing troupe of bohemian gypsies. A circle of red brick dust, large feathers wafting the smoke of burning incense, black candle at the boy's head, skulls, feathers, gem stones. A curious blend of art and science.

Kal was quick to take over, making adjustments for the ritual and preparing his mind. He shook the anxiety out of his hands and rubbed them together to get the tingles going. Blew into his fists, drummed on his chest, cracked his neck.

Mab stepped up behind him and placed a black top hat on his head, one of the old symbols of a voodoo king. He sat down in a tall-backed oak chair at the head of the table and felt the weight of that hat on his head, all that it meant and symbolized. This was suddenly very real.

"He have any footholds?"

"Catholic maybe."

"Assumptions ain't good enough," Mab muttered.

"Baseline subconscious gotta have the basic archetypes."

"Keep to the old loas."

Their inside jargon was like the banter of doctors diagnosing a malady except these doctors used the names of gods and the levels of hell and a bunch of strange occult lingo.

"Of course," Kal huffed as he assembled a series of bone tools on the table and stuffed a chunk of amethyst stone in his pocket. He paused and took several deep breaths. Mab's shop was a familiar sanctity, a kind of hallow ground for spirit work. Despite the nostalgia, it still reminded Kal of the rift between he and his Godmother.

Eden was still in shock. She sat in the corner and watched, feeling uncomfortable and twitchy. Mab offered her a thermos of tea to calm her nerves and she accepted it graciously, trying not to make eye contact. With each sip she prayed the bone masks wouldn't track her to this place. She had caused enough trouble already.

"Almost there," said Kal.

His eyes were closed and his breathing deep. This shop was a place of strength and roots, where he learned incantations and potion chemistry all those years ago. It was strong enough in his mind that he could dig in a foothold to the space and dangle his consciousness precariously into another person's dream. Crossing the barrier from his own subjective reality to another's—especially one who is sick or cursed—called for the highest level of clarity and focus. Kal was shit for both and hoped his guts and tenacity would be enough to carry him through as they always did.

"Just make it back to the candle," said Mab over his shoulder.

Kal opened his eyes to take one last look at the black candle's flame and whispered, "Begin."

Mab led with a steady patter on her hand drum that produced a loose, twangy vibration across the room. She paced the perimeter of the table waving the drum around as she beat it, as though she were shooing off unwanted pests. Donnie stood as a silent guardian and listened as the beat produced its hypnotic effect.

For Kal the drum beats were stairs descending along a spiral into somewhere far beneath his normal, waking mind. He followed and breathed, slowly disconnecting himself from his own body and surroundings.

The chanting and incense, strange skull candles, and oddly placed mirrors gave the atmosphere an eerie funhouse vibe that distorted the senses. A surreal pageant when fully enacted, the effect was the creation of a liminal space outside of time, disconnected from the world. It got colder in the room and the walls seemed further away.

Mab intoned a meandering chant as she circled and beat her drum.

"Hoya hoya ro ho ro ho...."

Kal swayed in the chair and let himself fall into the trance, deep down beneath his conscious thoughts in the river of intuition where the bullshit of the world fell away. The drum beat steps dissolved and opened up into a vast expanse of nothing. His mind let go of the bonds that kept him tied to people and plots and drama. Disconnected. Floating.

"...Ro ho ro ho... Hoya Hoya rishi rishi ho ho ..."

The nonsense syllables were further away now but continued to bring form to his thoughts, inviting protective faces and presences to see him through.   Sacred old ones and little helpers.   Static fuzz and Technicolor imagination.   There in the trance he began to feel the pull of the kid's soul.   His instincts pointed like a magnet finding north and his consciousness swam forward into the darkness.

"...Hoya ho ho Hoya ho ho..."

As He followed it and his mind slipped down the river, traveling through the hole in the static, Kal's soul tumbled to the other side.

Stillness gripped him and he took a breath.

Now comes the focus.   The balance.   The kung fu of spirit walking.

Kal hadn't done an honest-to-god soul retrieval in years and then only once. It was tricky. Like hanging upside down from your toes and painting a mandala in shifting sands.

When the stillness arrived, Kal opened his eyes.

The spirit world is different for everyone and takes many forms but it's generally disorienting.   Kal found himself in a subterranean corridor beneath a vaulted cave ceiling, surrounded by deep shadows and the potent smell of death.   Olin's soul was a faint glow trailing ahead in the darkness. Kal followed the thread across a wet, spongy terrain.

Foul winds rushed down the cave tunnel and punched at Kal from all sides and the edges of the world whipped about like a tattered flag. Everything fought for his attention, which flailed about wildly, but Kal trained his focus on that glowing light.

"Hoya hoya rishi rishi ro yo ro yo . . ."

The chant came from somewhere far away and was swallowed by the screaming wind but it helped to maintain the trance.

The cave narrowed and wound deep into the Earth (if that's where this was). As he gained on the trailing light of the fleeing soul, Kal noted the rock walls were etched with tribal meso-American murals. Depictions of animal-headed priests conducting mass sacrifice and hordes of warriors with demon masks lined the tunnel. Pools of blood, severed heads, and piles of bodies gave Kal enough clues to gather that this was the demesne of an ancient dark god. He swallowed hard and listened for Mab's voice on the violent wind.

"Mek, could you—" he stopped himself, remembering that his little friend had been blasted to spectral dust. The reminder stung and he put his head down to press on.

The winding tunnel soon opened into a large underground cavern illuminated in an eerie blood red light. The dome of the underground temple arched several stories into the air above and centered on a foul insignia Kal recognized all too well. Burned and carved into the center of the ceiling's arch was the horrible sigil he had seen tattooed on Eden's back, complete with a set of scowling eyes peering down at him.

"Looks like the right place," he said to no one but himself.

The real horror wasn't to be found on the ceiling however. A scan of the cave floor explained the mysterious glow bathing the place in red. All along the moist, mossy floor were vast swathes of glowing molten red egg sacks that lined the chamber like fish row in a pond.

Kal's first instinct was to be sick but he wrestled his guts into submission. The egg sacks pulsed and breathed in a constantly wobbling motion. The smell was wet and bloody and as Kal crept slowly and carefully along the nest of eggs, he caught sight of what was inside. Each of the eggs contained a little bug-eyed fetus resembling a distorted human baby.

This was more than a nest.

He looked to the dust at his feet, a familiar sooty grey powder that confirmed his fears. These were *souls*. The souls of Oblivion's victims.

There were hundreds of souls trapped here, in slimy little red bubbles, like a garden of eggs. Their bodies were shuffling around on the streets above like zombies but the real spirit stuff was someone's private collection. Kal had no idea el Brujan had already nabbed so many victims. This was worse than he thought.

The glow of Olin's floating soul caught his attention and Kal followed it to a plateau that rose up in the middle of the cavern. The little orange light was gently settling into position in a cluster of eggs where it began to embed itself in the nest, a red gelatin pod forming around it.

Kal quickly found a foothold on the plateau and climbed its porous surface.

That's when he heard the screech. The clicking coming closer. The smell.

This garden had a guardian.

Perfect.

Whatever monster was approaching through the wide tunnel mouth on the north side of the cavern made the walls shudder and the egg sacs quiver at its presence. It knew someone was here.

Kal had to act quickly. He scrambled up the side of the jagged plateau as fast as he could, the winds and noise around him like a hurricane as his panic escalated. Another screech and closer now, echoing off the walls. Kal slipped off a foothold and dangled on the rock wall.

The air was getting colder, his lungs tightening and as the chittering sounds of something with many legs grew closer, the egg sacks around him began to quiver and secrete some foul oil in anticipation or, perhaps, fear.

Kal focused his mind and narrowed his attention to the task at hand. The underworld was a tricky, horrible place if you let the sensations get to you. The kid's soul was just ahead. He found another foothold and clambered up the rocks to the plateau surface.

The surface of the mesa was just as spongy and crowded as the rest of the cavern but Kal reached the cluster of egg sacks where the faint light was settling into the goo. He couldn't touch the soul directly, it was too sensitive. The effect would be jarring to Olin. Instead he reached into his pocket and drew out the shard of amethyst.

As Kal coaxed the little light back into his gemstone for safe travel, the entire cave trembled violently. Kal looked up as rocks and dust fell from overhead. Then the screeching again.

"Come on, come on, come on..." he chanted as the glimmer of life carefully tucked itself into his stone.

As fortune would have it, another egg sac beckoned to Kal from nearby. His instincts were pointing to it, a kind of magnetic connection.

It dawned on him suddenly whose soul was in the pod. There was just enough time to sneak that other soul into the Amethyst.

Just as it sealed itself inside, something huge and slimy emerged from the tunnel across the cave causing the walls to tremble at its weight and the force of its charge. Kal looked up and all his favorite curse words failed him.

It was massive and terrible, a many-legged bulging behemoth of the cavernous underworld. The monster resembled a giant centipede on steroids, pumped up on hell's venom, and wiggling several hideous appendages in Kal's direction.

"Ah fuck."

That was enough to get his heart thumping. Kal slipped the glowing soul rock into his pocket and leaped over the edge of the plateau. The ten foot freefall through the spirit winds dizzied him and he landed on the squishy ground in a puddle of egg sac yuck.

There was no time for remorse at the squashed souls. The demon centipede exploded into motion and rattled across the cavern toward the fleeing spirit walker. Kal dashed like mad through the dust and muck in a bee-line for the tunnel that brought him in.

"Meklyn I could really use a—"

Mandibles crashed through a heap of rock just overhead, sending Kal rolling across the ground amidst heaps of debris. He scrambled to his feet.

Damnit, Meklyn, I need you!

The dire insect crashed after him, mandibles clicking and dripping with venom, both of them sending rocks and egg sacks flying across the cavern. Kal made a sprinting leap over a barrier of rubble to the far tunnel that led him in.

The worm snapped again and he felt the wind off that one. Had to roll to the side, crashing into a bundle of egg sacks that broke and oozed warm pus all over him. The smell made him gag and he held back the urge to wretch and vomit. Getting back to his feet and running was far more important.

The centipede screeched and lunged, narrowly missing Kal's leg as he dashed into the alcove.

The tunnel shook as he ran through the dark, listening through his own rapid breathing for Mab's chanting. Rocks fell from the tunnel ceiling and he leaped, rolled, dove out of the blast radius. The creature was plowing through the tunnel, tearing it apart in pursuit of the thief.

The black candle glowed in the darkness ahead, a beacon leading Kal home.

Wind whipped at his face, at the flame, at reality.

The mandibles reached for him. Licked the back of his neck. He pumped his legs harder.

The doorway was closing.

So close.

And then a rush of sound and light broke over him.

Kal broke through the barrier into the sacred space of Mab's shop just in time to slam the door behind him. A final screech echoed in his mind and he vomited violently across the table. Huge projected stream of red slimy spirit world bile.

He collapsed to the floor, out of breath.

The room fell to an eerie silence, the circle dropped and the magic gone in a cold deadened vacuum. Somewhere above, Olin coughed and gasped for breath. Mab rushed to his side and propped up his head. The kid choked, wheezed and rolled off the table to cough and sputter back to life on the floor next to his exhausted rescuer.

Relief washed over Kal and he laid there at rest.

"You okay, buddy?"

Kal's eyes were woozy and drunk as he looked up at the blurry image of Donnie's face.

"Fuck. That," Kal answered.

Donnie chuckled and lifted Kal to his feet.

Olin coughed and sputtered while Kal steadied himself from the dizziness. His senses took time to reorient to his surroundings. Returning to the rigid world of form was always more jarring than expected. Nothing physical had happened to his body while he was away, yet still he felt slimed and disgusting. His muscles ached from the fall, his eyes and ears had to adjust and as they did, he knew something had gone terribly wrong. The kid was fine. Olin was already starting to open his eyes, the color returning to his skin.

Something else.

"Where's Eden?"

TWENTY

SO MUCH NICER out here.

She stepped into the night air, smelled the midnight breeze, and tried to calm down. Thoughts raced through her head at high velocity, many of which she'd rather weren't there. The soul retrieval Kal was doing had started to get strange. He was twisting around in some kind of seizure, murmuring and moaning. Some foul presence wrapped around the room and she felt little bugs crawling all over her. It just made sense to get out of there.

What was Eden to these people anyway? *A liability?* *A sick patient?* She wasn't sure anymore. The thoughts rambled on and continued to confuse her.

She turned a corner and expected to find . . .

Well, she wasn't exactly sure what she expected to find. In fact, she wasn't entirely sure where she was. How had she gotten here?

Eden, what are you doing out wandering around?

The rational faculties in her mind had shut down and she followed her rambling chattering thoughts out into the night, not even realizing she was walking right into—

"Evening, Sweetness."

A host of skull-faced soldiers emerged from the darkness around her and a heavy boot smashed the protective skull that warded the cobblestone street. Eden's heart shifted to a desperate thundering and her lungs sealed up.

The tall, wraith-like Bael stepped from the ranks and smiled beneath his red lenses.

Eden's voice caught in her throat and she couldn't even scream. It had been a mind trick, a trap. She'd played right into it.

Stupid, Eden! Stupid! But it was too late.

Hands seized her from all sides and her struggles were pointless. The Brujan soldiers crammed her into the back seat of one of their jet black Broncos and peeled off into the night. The stress and the mind magic that seized her throat from making any sound finally cut her off and she passed out completely.

The disappearing tail lights reflected in Bael's red lenses and he gave his men the nod for Phase Two.

KAL THREW OPEN the door to give what he knew would be a fruitless chase to the car that was already speeding away with Eden. But there was no need. Two Brujan soldiers met him at the threshold, leering skull faces inches away and gleaming Desert Eagles in their hands.

There was no time for words. Kal jumped back and threw the door closed but the soldiers were already stomping past the protective wards.

"Mab, get out now!"

Kal's words trailed off in an echo as the reverberation of a silencer spit two bullets into his belly.

"Kal!"

He heard Donnie's voice far away and a strange laugh haunted him from the shadows around the room. The screeching creature. The winds of the underworld. Kal stumbled back and the events around him became a blur.

Donnie saw his friend take two to the gut and something snapped in his brain. He went full blown ape shit. Gun was in his hand at a reflex and *BOOM BOOM BOOM* he sent lead soaring across the room.

Chunks of wood exploded all around the shop and the kid from La Jolla started screaming under the table as the room literally exploded into chaos overhead.

Donnie grabbed Mab and ducked beneath the large oak table, the wall of tribal masks behind them erupting with the spray of bullet holes. He fired another few rounds at the soldiers' feet. One shot clipped a calf muscle and the guy hit the floor with a groan but his buddy was already zipping around the perimeter and two more of their group slipped in the front windows.

Mab got to Kal's side and sat him up. His eyes were still wide and in shock, blood gurgling in his throat. That dark laughter called to him from the windy shadows.

"Mab, can you—?" Donnie started to ask but panic was creeping into his voice.

"Ye mind the gunfire," she said, setting to work.

Donnie didn't hesitate. He was more comfortable spilling blood than stitching it up. He squeezed the trigger and sent his rage zipping across the room at the black shadows ducking and weaving along the perimeter.

One soldier tried to balance his back against a door jamb only to have the wards etched into the wood burst to flame around him and suddenly he was on fire, yelling to his comrades for help.

Mab gave Kal two hard slaps on the stomach and placed her hand patiently at his mouth, whispering and murmuring prayers to the gods. It seemed to take longer than she expected but suddenly Kal was coughing up the bullets and sputtering to breathe.

"That's it, boy, now take a big breath," she said. He looked up at her and his gaze was far away. "Don't ye go slippin' back to the spirit realm on me, damnit. Breathe!"

She slammed him hard in the chest and Kal took a deep inhale, the air a cold shock to his lungs.

He coughed and sputtered, the room taking on solid form again. The laughter in the shadows began to fade and he found Mab's eyes.

"Mab . . ."

"Best be gettin' out of here," she said.

Bullets burst into the couch near their heads and Kal's senses sharpened.

Donnie was still close by.

"Stand still, freaks!" his friend was shouting as he fired round after round into darting shadows. The soldiers were like wraiths. Suddenly two were behind Donnie grabbing his arms and pinning his motion.

They almost had him disarmed when Kal found his footing and made a hard line drive into their waists. A whole pile of bodies rolled across the floor, knocking over furniture and spilling potion bottles from the shelves.

Mists and vapors erupted into a cloud around them sending the boys into fits of coughing and choking. Kal laid a swift punch to the first soldier and wrestled Donnie free.

"Kal!"

Donnie's warning was quick and Kal ducked as a black dagger swished past his neck.

In the scuffle he palmed a silver potion vial and tossed it at the backstabber.

The liquid splashed against the attacker's mask and a swarm of mosquitos took form in the silver mist. The swarm cocooned the attacker in a hive of hungry insects. He swatted and stumbled as the swarm grew, overpowering him and wrestling him to the floor amidst painful screaming.

Donnie kicked the other soldier square in the belly and sent him stumbling into his flaming comrade. The two skull-clad soldiers landed on the maroon suede couch and the thing burst into flames.

Fire, bullets and the scuffle found the boys finally on their feet side by side. Olin was still screaming and Mab found her footing in the corner. One soldier fired at her and she instinctively swatted the bullets aside, her face a dangerous scowl.

"Curse ye unborn and Guedhe have yer souls!" she spat with a venom that rivaled the flame in her eyes. Shapes emerged from the floorboards and wrapped around the Brujan soldiers. Twisted, black shapes that tore at the invaders and hissed like steam vents. The men behind the masks screamed and fought but it was no use. The witch had laid her curse and now the cultists knew only suffering.

"Come on, this way!" Mab shouted and the guys followed. Kal bent beneath the table to coax Olin to follow.

"Let's go, kid, now!"

Olin was in complete shock and the only thing that convinced him to follow was the fear of staying. First he's snorting a new drug, then a nightmare he couldn't even describe, and he wakes up to a shootout in a burning building with nasty spirits bubbling up from the ground. His mind was close to shutting down from the trauma.

He followed Kal and the others through the front lobby as the place began to catch fire all around them, flames spreading along the ancient shelves and the soldiers wrestling desperately with tormenting spirit guardians.

A small crowd of neighbors had already gathered on the street outside and they collectively gasped when Mab and the boys emerged from the little shop of flames and gunfire.

"Mab, honey!"

A young woman rushed to Mab's side and helped her across the street, age finally showing in the formidable woman's gait. A few men crowded around Kal and the guys, helping them to safety as the screams of the Brujan soldiers still cried out from inside the shop.

"Over here!"

"You boys okay?"

The sound of sirens grew in the distance and, in the commotion, Mab turned to see her shop in flames. The look on her face hit Kal harder than the gunshots to the gut. That was her home, her temple. And it was burning because of him. He brought this to her doorstep.

There was no more thinking.

Kal broke from the crowd and dashed into the shop.

"Kal, what the—"

Donnie's voice faded and there was only the fire.

The soldiers were fighting to get to the back door but the guardian spirits had nearly won, that ravaging black smoke having all but consumed them of flesh and soul. Kal looked around in a mad rush and quickly found the fire extinguisher.

He fumbled with it. Hell, had he even used one of these before?

The instructions were like Greek and he fidgeted with the hose. Finally he whispered low and steady to the shop.

"Amon Ra Ga'ran."

The extinguisher burst to life in his hands, flailing and spouting massive white clouds of coolant across the walls of licking flames. He painted the whole shop with the stuff, dousing the fire even as the guardian spirits receded back into the floorboards and the Brujan soldiers withered into corpses on the floor.

A silence, deep and heavy, fell over the shop when the fire was out.

Sirens grew closer.

Kal attempted a deep breath but spun into a fit of violent coughing. His stomach ached from the wound that was haphazardly patched. His mind was still sore and reeling from the spirit walk. The shop he once called home was nearly a charred husk. And Mab . . .

Kal came out to the astonishment of the crowd and stood there before them a moment.

Suddenly the weight of all his deeds stared back at him from a dozen different faces.

Suddenly he was on display.

Judged.

Donnie leaned against the Jag across the street and gave his buddy a reassuring nod.

Turning to look at the shop, Kal saw the years of his life in the smoking husk of that old occult store. A thousand haunted questions knocked at the doors of his mind.

Where did he come from? Why was he like this? The gods had never given him any answers, only more questions. Was he the sinner or the saint? Medicine Maker or Poisoner? Or some kind of both?

Kal found Mab at the front of the crowd and crossed to her.

"Mab, I'm... *I'm sorry.*"

She gazed hard at him for a long, uncomfortable moment. Years passed in a single look. Then she placed a hand on his cheek.

"Yer a good medicine man. But ye got a helluva mess to clean up."

There was a long pause as Kal processed it all. She was cold. But she said exactly what he needed to hear in that moment. He kissed her forehead and plodded through the crowd.

He met Donnie at the Jag without a word. Donnie slapped him on the back and they loaded into the car. The car sped around the corner and out of sight as the blaring sirens of the first responders arrived.

The wind whipped in through the car, smacking them with the cold night air, and Donnie looked over at Kal.

"What's next?"

Kal thought for a moment.

"I can find 'em."

Donnie nodded. "And then?"

Kal returned his gaze and said with a voice as firm as stone, "Who do we know that will go to war with us?"

TWENTY-ONE

EDEN WAS SCARED, more so than ever before.

It wasn't the long, silent ride or the armed necromancers that gave her the chills. It was the suspense. It might have been easier if she didn't know what her captors could do, if she hadn't witnessed firsthand the sort of hell in which they trafficked. But she did. And she had.

The entourage of black SUVs bumped and jostled along a deep back road that snaked across a barren landscape toward the Brujan compound. She watched the desert pass by, memories of her desperate escape flickering in the back of her head, how far she'd gotten before they finally found her.

Their caravan pulled in to its destination outside a squat little ranch house with a large red barn rising from the field behind it. Eden's captors didn't move right away, waiting for orders in the bronco, engine off, windows up. It was Bael that jerked the car door open with a predatory glee.

"Welcome back," he said with a grin that nearly swallowed his already pinched face. Bael's blonde hair seemed always to be combed back perfectly, angular neck and prominent cheek bones jutting out to give him an all but reptilian appearance.

Eden refused to make eye contact, even through those obnoxious red sunglasses. Xechan was certainly the boss around here but there was something about "*Lieutenant*" Bael that made her skin crawl. The trouble with most people was their overwhelming thoughts that blared like trumpets in Eden's ears and paraded through her mind. His mind, however, was a curious vacuum. Even *el Diablo* had thoughts raging around him but Bael was a Sphinx guarding a black hole. She ignored his arrogantly extended hand and found her own footing to step from the vehicle.

The Brujan Lieutenant held to his smug grin as he led her up the front steps of the house, a trio of leering skeletal masks with high powered machine guns following closely behind to make sure she followed obediently. It was a small farmhouse with a front porch somewhere in East County with a sparse desert that boxed them in for miles around. The lot was still and quiet, except for the dozens of Brujan soldiers stalking the fields like ghosts. The whole property was crawling with them, Xechan's own private army.

Bael led her into the house through the dark front room and turned down a hall toward the bedroom.

Eden froze. Her heart began to race, her mind to wander. The soldiers nudged her along but her legs rebelled.

"No!" she roared and turned to bolt but the hall was too cramped. They grabbed Eden and dragged her kicking and struggling into the bedroom.

"Leggo, stop it!" she grunted furiously.

What would they do?   How would they do it?

"No! No!" went her screams as she pounded on them with her fists.

Reaching the bed, Bael's men forced Eden to her knees and tied her to the bedpost with little thought to gentleness. When control of her muscles failed she tried to reign in her tempestuous thoughts but they raced to terrible places.

Bael leaned in close, Eden's own red reflection staring back at her from his lenses.

"Your punishments will be various," he whispered menacingly in her ear.

A thousand horrific things sprang to Eden's mind, like an avalanche of poison dumped straight into her brain. She howled and spat in Bael's smug face.

Bael's mouth twitched, a swift lick of the lips, and he calmly—slowly—wiped the spit from his cheek and smeared it on the young woman's forehead. Without another word the men left her alone in the dark. Eden trembled and fought back the sobs. She tried to wiggle loose but the knots were strong. Her mind was shaky and confused, like she'd been drugged or, she supposed, *cursed*.

TWENTY-TWO

DONNIE'S BLACK JAG pulled slowly up a private drive to a massive three-story cabin overlooking the mountains outside of Julian. It was just after four in the morning but lights were still burning in the rustic mansion.

"You sure about this?" Donnie asked for the third or fourth time.

"Got another idea?"

Donnie took a breath and surveyed the line of beefy security guards filing out of the garage toward his car. They were the biggest and meanest the Krank Street Krew had to offer and this was an uninvited surprise visit.

"This better work or we're fish food, Kal."

Donnie rolled his window down and found a gun barrel a few inches from his nose.

"Fuck you doin' here, DeGrassi?"

"Important business with Dre," was all Donnie said, hands in full view.

Within moments they had been jerked from the car and herded into the garage with guns digging into their backs. Donnie couldn't help but continue to give Kal uncertain, challenging looks as if to remind him that this absurd gambit was his idea.

Kal was a stone-cold stoic. He was nervous but a few gun-toting gangbangers weren't half as terrifying as the hell he'd already seen tonight. He let things play out however they would. About as Zen as he could be in the face of all this.

After some shouting and stomping around upstairs, Dre came tromping down the staircase and into the drafty garage where his visitors were waiting patiently at gunpoint.

"You got some balls comin' here, Doc."

"Look, Dre—" Donnie started.

"You know better, motherfucka, I don't want to hear what you got to say!"

"Just hear me out," Kal insisted.

Dre always had the itchy trigger-finger look to him and right now he was practically foaming at the mouth to take his anger and frustration out on someone. Kal tried not to think about it.

"I'm listening," Dre growled.

Kal slowly pulled the chunk of purple amethyst from his pocket and held it up in the dim light. Dre looked around at his Krew and couldn't decide whether to laugh or shoot this idiot.

"Is this a joke?" he demanded. "You came up here to my private pad to show me a goddamn rock?"

"You give me five minutes, I can cure Reese."

The Kranks passed anxious and uncertain looks around the garage. They were desperate for a cure for their cousin but Dre couldn't afford to lose face with this.

"Why should I trust you?"

Dead stare, Kal replied, "Because your boy's straight out of the Walking Dead in there. What do you got to lose?"

Like a reflex, Dre lunged at Kal, stopping nose-to-nose with him and daring him to keep talking with those carnage-hungry eyes. Caught between his own Krew and a punk chemist he never liked all that much, Dre felt the pinch of the tension in the room. Kal stared back, unthreatening, waiting.

"You got 5 minutes. You hurt ma boy—"

"I won't."

Reluctantly and still itching to flay the skin from the medicine man's bones, Dre Daggers led him into a secure room upstairs where two teenage cousins and somebody's mother were tending to Reese in his... state. Poor guy didn't look much better. They had him stretched out on a futon where he just sort of squirmed absently, his skin still a putrid grey and his eyes rolled back into his head.

Kal and Donnie waited respectfully while Dre cleared the attendants out of the room. It took him a few minutes to convince the woman who seemed to be an aunt of some kind that it was alright. She gave Kal a death glare on her way out of the room and when it was quiet again, Dre motioned for Kal to get to work with whatever he was going to do.

Getting one last look of warning and encouragement from Donnie, Kal approached Reese's bedside and cleared his mind for the work. He wasn't entirely sure how this would go but Olin didn't seem to have problems. Carefully, he placed the amethyst down on the night stand near Reese's head and took a step back.

Almost immediately the zombied body jerked into a violent spasm as his nervous system synced up with the disconnected soul deep inside the folded atoms of the purple stone.

Kal winced as quick flashes of that subterranean prison and that many-legged beast tore through his mind. The smell of death and decay filled the room along with a shrill, ear-piercing whine that came roaring out of the stone along with a thick black smoke. Everyone in the room recoiled and stepped back as Kal did his best to block out the sound and kneel down beside Reese.

Dre was itchy and started toward Kal but Donnie held him back. "Wait, man, just wait! Trust me, Andre! Trust me!"

Kal watched the spirit smoke swirl around Reese's body, billowing out of the stone. It only just occurred to him that this soul had been gone much longer than Olin's. There could be... *complications*. He placed a hand on the victim's forehead and whispered prayers to the more benevolent deities that roamed the higher planes.

Reese's body started to shake and convulse as the smoke circled them. Howling ghosts swirled around in the cloud, shrieking and moaning, sending chills down every spine in the room. Kal was caught in the middle of the storm too, struggling to maintain focus as the little nasties of the nether worlds ripped and pulled at his flesh and his hair and his mind.

"Kal?!" Donnie called out just to check.

Kal was miles away, however, muttering his prayers and feeling the revolting energy run through poor Reese's twitching body.

After all the loud wailing and the storm of the abyss crashing around in the air, suddenly and finally it all went quiet. Reese's body went limp and the gemstone went dark.

Nothing.

"What happened?" Dre demanded in the echo of the ensuing silence.

Nobody moved. Reese wasn't moving at all and, for a moment, Kal was terrified that his plan had backfired.

Shit...

"Goddamnit, freak, what did you do to ma cousin!?"

Dre was pouncing before Donnie could contain him. He bowled Kal over and they wrestled across the floor as the room erupted into shouting and wrestling.

"Dre! No!"

"Wait!"

"Get off of him!"

The Kranks grabbed Donnie and held him back.

"Kill him, Dre!"

"The fuck he do?!"

Dre pinned Kal's arms down and the other Kranks piled up on Donnie to hold him in the far corner.

"Stop it, Dre!" Donnie shouted, almost feral as he struggled helplessly to get to his friend. "Damn it, man, just stop a minute!"

With a flick of his wrist, Dre Daggers had a giant serrated knife in his hand and he raised it menacingly over Kal's throat.

"I warned you, freak!"

Suddenly there was coughing and a choking scream behind Dre as Reese burst to life and gasped for air. His awakening was followed by a terrified wail as though he had just awoken from the most horrible nightmare he'd ever had.

He screamed and babbled incoherently, backing up against the wall and looking around for the night terrors that had haunted him.

"NO NO STOP! STOP!! Let me go!" he shouted. "Please don't—AGH!"

His cousins crowded around him and whispered calming words, coaxing Reese out of the nightmare and back to Earth. It took a few minutes to get him calmed down, like waking a man from a sleepwalking dream, and Dre kept his knife at Kal's throat the whole time.

Kal had already accepted that if this was a fail on his part, he was dead. He waited patiently, listening to Reese's groans and babbling. He'd done all he could do. It was in the hands of the Gods now.

When the kid finally calmed down enough to realize where he was and who was around him, he caught his breath and cried.

"Thank you God, thank you God..." he repeated over and over again, sobbing into his bewildered cousin's hoodie.

Dre looked down at Kal with mixed emotions. He sheathed the dagger and crossed to Reese's bed.

"Reese, man," he said with a soft tone. "You alright?"

Reese pulled out of his breakdown and wiped the slime from his face. "Goddamnit, Dre. I d-don't know where I was man but... God don't let me g-go back there!"

The poor kid could only lower his head and breathe as the visceral horror of being a larval plaything in that demon-critter's cave slowly worked its way out of his system. Donnie helped Kal to his feet and they stood on the sidelines waiting and watching. After a few minutes at his cousin's side, Dre stood and straightened himself up before crossing the room.

"I owe you an apology," he said. It wasn't easy for him to say, but he did. "Thank you."

Ever the bigger man, Kal simply nodded.

"He gonna be alright?"

"As far as I can tell," Kal answered. "Might be sick for a few days and he'll need some counseling to get over what he's been through."

Dre nodded, trying to understand what the hell just happened.

"It ain't over yet," Donnie added.

The look of war returned to Dre's eyes and he was back to his senses.

"Just tell me what we gotta do."

Donnie and Kal exchanged an ominous glance. They knew it wouldn't be easy.

TWENTY-THREE

IT SEEMED LIKE HOURS went by as she fought to keep her drooping head up. Finally, amidst the white noise and confusion, Eden heard the back screen door.

The room felt heavy with the quiet. Expectant. It was as though the space prepared itself for the man who drew near. His footsteps fell heavy in the hallway. Eden held her breath as Xechan strode calmly across the faded green carpet and towered over her like a specter. He wasn't adorned in any imposing ritual garb this time. No, he was the man she remembered. The alluring rebel that had seduced her. Barefoot and shirtless, a statue of muscle and jagged ink.

She gulped a lump in her throat as he placed his fingers lightly under her chin and lifted her gaze to meet his eyes. Eden recoiled at the sight of him. He pulled her gaze again, a snake charming its helpless prey and she shivered uncontrollably.

"Do not be afraid, my queen," Xechan whispered in a low growl.

She looked at him. At the monster. His nostrils flared like some beast and he surveyed her like prey, completely calm and still.

"I've missed you," he said.

"You can have my body, you monster, but you'll never—"

He slapped her hard across the face and she was silenced.

Xechan leaned in and whispered in her ear, an intimacy that made her ache and shudder.

"You are a temple now. A Gate. A much greater purpose than a whore."

The man stood and stalked from the room. Eden heard the screen door slam and she burst into tears. Feeling helpless was part of her despair but the suspense—her imagination—was the real torture.

TWENTY-FOUR

A DARK NIGHT SKY blanketed the desert around the black Jag. Donnie leaned against it, smoking his last clove as three sets of headlights made their way down County Road 29. The vehicles pulled off the road and formed a semi-circle around Donnie before they cut their engines. Car doors opened releasing dozens of boots to the parched sand.

He had wondered how many would show. He sent the word out on every encrypted twitter and bounced text ring he knew. Only two clans showed an interest in a little retaliation strike besides the Kranks. Three crazy gangs of assholes who never turned down a good fight.

"This is your army?"

Dre Daggers stalked forward. He had six of his guys with him, each one a walking arsenal of black market scraps. Uzis, Berettas, Tasers, serrated knives, brass knuckles, and a couple of not-fucking-around AK-47s. The Kranks lived for this gangbanger shit. Donnie gave them a nod and scanned the other soldiers.

From a VW van spray-painted with violent lewd cartoons and splatter graffiti emerged a crew of eight punk rock clowns who went out of their way to earn the clan name Psychedelic Hooligans. They spent most of their time in an underground brew lab or the Kit Carson skate park but when a chance to cause trouble scratched their radar, these merry pranksters followed a skinny Mexican kid they called Hoolio into battle.

Hoolio had prepared them for war. Obnoxious clown makeup covered their scowling (some smiling) faces and they were almost certainly packing jacket loads of grenades and flammable aerosol cans in those baggy pockets of theirs. Hoolio ignored Dre completely and gave Donnie a silent nod, which was respectfully returned.

Finally there were the Gear Heads. Darby and his three biggest, meanest bruisers stepped to the circle, towering over the others by a foot or two. For these guys a brawl was a brawl. They carried crow bars and metal bats for getting up close, their firearms stowed as a last resort.

Donnie flicked his cigarette butt. "Big happy family."

"Don't know how big it is," Dre said, eyeing the group aggressively. "But I wouldn't miss this shit."

Darby growled defensively.

"Thanks for coming," Donnie said. "All of you."

A couple of the Kranks had some difficulty maintaining their game face as the Hooligan clowns kept turning slowly to smile at them with a creepy leer.

"Been too long since we thinned out the herd," Dre continued to taunt.

"It's been a while since anyone broke the truce, it's true," Donnie said, keeping things as calm and focused as possible. "But this isn't about us. Or our own rivalries. These ass clowns—no offense—"

Hoolio shrugged.

"—aren't part of our pacts or truces," Donnie went on. "El Brujan's a foreign invader and they've insulted us. Threatened our way of doin' business. All of us. That's why we're meeting tonight. As allies."

Donnie paused to see if his rallying speech was having any noticeable effect. So far his sentiments seemed to set well with everyone. Moving right along.

"After tonight we'll be able to go back to—"

"What's the plan?" Darby interrupted impatiently.

"Kill 'em all," Dre cut in with a laugh echoed by his Krew.

The Hooligans all cracked silent grins and nodded. Donnie was losing their attention.

"Alright alright, we all got bloodlust, I get it," he said, stalling. "Before we go in guns blazing, let's keep a few things in mind. First—"

Donnie's warnings were interrupted again, this time by a violent coughing fit from somewhere behind him on the rocky hill. The gangs exchanged confused glances as a lone figure stumbled down out of the night, pounding his chest as he hacked and sputtered like an aged Marlboro Man.

Kal made his way toward them, finally taking shape in the pale moonlight. He finished his little episode by hacking a righteous loogie onto the ground at Dre's feet.

"Ugh," Kal groaned, catching his breath and shaking off the fit. "Gotta lay off the pipe."

"Kal?" Donnie inquired with a raised eyebrow.

Kal waved him off and began to pace as he spoke. "Right right, so before we hike across that field, I should warn you. There's more than guns and knives over there."

"They got bombs 'n shit too?" asked one of the Kranks.

"More like black magic," Kal replied with that mad look in his eyes.

He half expected the typical response of rolling eyes and arrogant sneers but all of them had seen the darkness first hand in the past few days so no one batted an eye. There was some nervous shuffling but he had their attention. Kal continued his pacing.

"I been scouting the compound for hours now. Made several passes overhead. Main activity centers on the barn. Looks like that's where they brew. Guys in the black robes are the ones to watch out for, they'll get inside your head if you're not careful. The soldiers are positioned around the perimeter and stalk the grounds in pairs. AKs on all of 'em."

Some more anxious shifting. They heard him right. An army of assault rifles and voodoo.

"There's something else too," Kal said. "I'm not sure what it is, something down below, underground. Could be a problem. Stay sharp."

"Thanks, Dad," quipped Dre. "Somebody got a plan?"

"Sure do, son, now shut the fuck up and listen," Donnie grumbled.

Kal ignored Dre's offended posturing and began laying out his strategy to an attentive audience, drawing a battle plan in the sand as he spoke. The Krank Street boys would strike first, down on the south border of the property, drawing forces and primary attention away from the barn so the Hooligans could nuke that place to hell, set it ablaze and hopefully purge some of the curses and wards hanging around the grounds. Odds are, that's where they were brewing the Oblivion so they could knock that stuff out, two birds one stone.

Darby's gang would keep a path to the house clear and mow down anything lingering in the ensuing chaos but the house belonged to Kal and Donnie. He was sure that's where the boss man was keeping Eden, all for himself and all alone. Anything goes wrong, they make a beeline for the main road and meet back at the cars.

When Kal finished explaining, and made it through another coughing fit that resulted in puddles of black tar hacked on the ground, the assembled warriors seemed satisfied, if a little repulsed by the Medicine Man's unabashed sickness. Guns were cocked and bats slapped open palms.

"When this is all done," Darby called over the scattered voices, quieting the mob once more. "We leave no trace of these bastards. Cut 'em all down for good and then we all get the fuck out."

"Done," said Donnie, finalizing the whole thing by cocking his pistol.

The groups went their separate ways, cutting across a large field of rocky dunes toward the ranch a half mile away.

Donnie and Kal slipped off to the right of the Gear Heads to climb the tallest hill overlooking the Brujan compound where they could oversee the initial phase. Kal kept his coughing in check as he tried to attune his senses to the energies of this place. The perimeter was cloaked in strange frequencies and he knew the Brujan priests would sense the attack if they weren't careful.

"You nervous?" Donnie asked.

"Shitting my pants," said Kal.

That got a chuckle from them both.

"Just like old times," said Donnie, glancing around warily.

"Not something to celebrate," Kal muttered.

They reached the peak and looked down over the compound. The barn was lit by a bright flood light affixed to a weather vane. A raging bonfire burned north of the house surrounded by robed figures that lurked in the dark shadows at its edge.

"How many you think we'll lose?" Kal asked.

"Does it matter?"

Kal had no response. They settled into position atop the ridge and waited for the next phase.

The Kranks had found a little spot next to an old camper in the weeds south of the red misshapen barn that rose like a monolith from the desert expanse. Big piles of junk gave them plenty of cover to prepare their initial assault. A pair of Brujan soldiers stalked the perimeter of the compound in their direction and two more stood watch at the south end of the barn. Their skull faces were all the more haunting in the pale light of the moon.

On the hill, Kal suddenly leaned forward.

"Look."

Donnie peered through the darkness to the bonfire where the hooded priests loitered. Two of them were bringing a struggling figure from the barn. The Brujan forced their captive to the ground, body and face covered by a black sacrificial robe, hands bound behind the back.

"Is that her?" Donnie asked.

Kal was already moving down the hill.

"Kal!"

Dre waited for the right moment, holding his itchy trigger finger still as long as possible, watching as the soldiers grew closer. Finally he gave the signal and they opened fire.

The *RAT TAT TAT* riddled the two sentries with bullets and echoed across the compound.

That was hell's cue to break loose.

The heads of Brujan soldiers and priests turned by the dozens and orders were shouted in angry Spanish. Black armored marksmen came running across the compound and with a collective battle cry the Kranks made it rain.

Automatic gunfire split the night and the place became a battlefield.

Bodies exploded in showers of blood that soaked the parched sand as the Kranks peppered the first ranks of their skull-faced enemies. The surprise caught at least five soldiers off guard and they dropped like lifeless meat sacks. Dre's guys took out the first wave with ease but it didn't take long for the cartel to regroup and turn the tables. Gun smoke and dust rose like a fog of death over the shoot-out as both sides let lead fly.

"Over there!"

Brujan forces emerged from the shadows in all directions and advanced like hungry ghosts.

"Watch that flank, Obie!" Dre called.

A Brujan soldier slipped out of the darkness like smoke and slashed with a gleaming sword through the neck of the warrior they called Obie. His head slid to the sand and brought looks of outrage to the Krew as he dropped. That was enough to send them into a blood frenzy.

"Obie!"

Bullets flew and screams of rage filled the night.

Kal and Donnie barreled over the hill toward the bonfire on the north side of the house. The priests were in formation around the fire, a black dagger held high over their prisoner, and all Kal could do was sprint, charging up his energy for a fight as he ran.

The diversion drew the mighty *Diablo* out onto the front porch of the house. He wore dark pants and his skull mask but his chest was bare to display the elaborate tattoos and scars. Kal came to a dead stop when he saw him and Xechan turned to stare. The feedback of the two conjure men created a ripple in the ether and Kal felt the ground spin beneath him. Xechan stared menacingly, probing at Kal's mind for information, for defenses... or maybe just to taunt him.

Gunfire ripped across the night.

"Let's go," Kal said and they were moving.

Xechan issued orders to his lieutenants and disappeared into the house.   Kal and Donnie broke down the hill and across the sand as a cadre of robed priests hurried to join the bonfire behind the house, their skeletal masks gleaming purple and red in the firelight.   They weren't the gun-toting arm of el Brujan. They were the real firepower.

Kal could already feel the static charge in the air as the priests shook a black powder out over the flames and began to circle the pit counter-clockwise. The world contorted to make room for their hex, a glitch in the Matrix that put Kal off balance and he stumbled.

"What's wrong?" Donnie asked but Kal was watching the skeletal brujos link up around the fire and begin their growling chant.

"AMAK ooRANI mah HAWTHam Du CROIX..."

The fire died down low while gunfire continued to pop in the background. A foul wind rolled over the desert. The hairs on Kal's body stood on end and a dizziness washed over them all, the kind of swimming stomach feeling you get right before an earthquake.

"Kal?"

"Eden!" Kal shouted, watching as the dagger lingered over her covered face.

The victim turned to look and the priest with the knife pulled the hood off.

Relief nearly bowled Kal over. It wasn't Eden. It was—

"Miles!" Donnie shouted.

They both started forward but knew they wouldn't make it over there in time. But that wasn't the worst of it. At the edge of his mind, Kal felt something move and a realization dawned on him. He knew what the priests were about to do.

Donnie pulled his pistol and ran toward the bonfire some 60 yards away. He was joined by the trio of giants slipping out of the shadows along the hillside. Darby and his guys followed Donnie's sprint across the grounds but it was too late. Miles gave Donnie one last pleading look of terror before the blade sunk deep into his neck and the circle of cultists leaped in the air with a shout.

Blood spewed from Miles' jugular and Donnie roared in anguish as he opened fire.

"Miles!"

Bullets sprayed across the night until the Earth itself suddenly gave a violent shake that sent them all stumbling.

"What the hell?" Darby shouted, scanning the area eagerly for enemies.

Kal didn't bother to answer. He wouldn't have to. The rumbling in the ground grew to a violent shaking beneath their feet and a rift of sand parted near the center of the compound. Then another nearby.

"Watch your step!" Kal called ominously.

The cultists dispersed into the night in multiple directions as the tremors grew to a deadly rumble that shook everyone to their feet. The ground displaced, the shaking, the static tremors in the air, Donnie's eyes became saucers when he realized what was happening.

"There's something down there!"

Something was moving through the ground. Something big.

"Keep moving," Kal warned as he caught up to Donnie and continued toward the small house. He was sorry for Miles but relieved that it hadn't been Eden. His resolve solid, there was only the house where the devil had disappeared. A soldier came around the corner and raised his gun at Kal's advance but one of the Gear Heads reacted with an axe that tumbled end over end into the attacker's grinning skull. They kept the pace of their advance, Donnie's burning rage and lust for vengeance driving him harder now. A fleeing cultist went darting by and Donnie filled him with lead, shouting his own curses at the murderer.

Near the barn, a group of small, quiet figures slipped through the night undetected. The Hooligans tip toed along the edge of the barn, an odd little gang of space clowns with grinning faces and hands full of explosives. The group hoisted two of their more agile bombers up the side of the barn to a ledge that peeked inside. The others fanned out into strategic positions and waited for Hoolio's signal.

As the enemy soldiers continued to make a run for the south border to engage the Kranks, an opening was left for the bomb squad.

The Brujan priests scattered across the compound. Their allies inside the barn held a solid guard of six or seven strong, set up to protect whatever was inside from the invaders.

Except nothing was safe from the Hooligans.

Hoolio was out first, spraying Uzi bullets into the soldiers guarding the entrance to the barn, raking the walls with splattered blood. His team was quick to follow, each making an excited hoot or battle cry as they lobbed grenades and homemade explosives into the barn.

BOOM! BOOM! POW!

The place burst into an explosion of light and fire that roared skyward in the night. Debris went flying, kicking up smoke and dust, and fire fanned out around the structure.

The suddenness of it brought a temporary hush over the compound.

The Hooligans laughed and hooted, lobbing a second round of fiery cocktails through the upper windows to explode in the recessed corners but their joy was short-lived.

In the wake of the explosions, the barn burning like a great signal fire, they too began to feel the tremors in the earth. Another rift parted the sands as something very large moved below ground, displacing the surface dirt.

Hoolio's eyes shot to the size of dinner plates and he bellowed for his team to, "RUN!"

It was too late.

As one of the Hooligans broke into a run, dodging a rain of gunfire, the ground beneath him exploded into the sky and an eight foot maw of razor sharp teeth tore out of the ground to swallow him whole.

Black and red rings erupted from the ground as a massive unholy hell worm protruded into the sky with the struggling Hooligan in its mouth.

Shock gave way to panic as everyone on the compound broke into a mad scramble.

Pandemonium surged away from the fifty foot snake like a ripple effect.

"Sweet Christ!" cried Darby, his men recoiling in horror at the sight.

Kal stared long and hard at the beast. Watched it chew and swallow a man and then dive back into the Earth to give chase to the others fleeing in every direction. That was a legit *hellworm*. One of the most ancient and deadly beasts of the Pit. This was no amateur cult of wannabe spell slingers. El Brujan was for real.

"Eden," he reminded himself. "Let's go!"

Kal led Donnie and the bewildered Gear Heads across the front lawn to the house. The shootout was a fucktastic mess of death and voodoo and carnage. Guns blasting, cars exploding, a demonic sand worm moving through the ground swallowing guys whole. The sky was red from the glow of the burning barn and the wails of strange spirits screamed across the windy terrain. Gunfire and screams collided with the ravaging destruction of that otherworldly snake that ripped from the Earth in one place and then another, gouging and striking at the gangsters and soldiers alike.

One of the priests came running from the side of the house, firing wildly at Kal.

Darby's biggest guy clocked him with the spade of a shovel and the cultist fell unconscious to the dirt.

Kal gave him an appreciative nod and bounded up the front steps, Donnie close behind.

"Keep a perimeter," he told the Gear Heads.

Kal and Donnie breached the house and found it deserted. Completely empty and eerily quiet.

"Goddamnit," Donnie said. "I did *not* see that coming."

Kal nodded grimly. "I'm sorry about Miles."

"Let's find this psycho."

Xechan had just dipped inside and couldn't have gotten far but it was dark and eerily quiet inside the house. Guns at the ready, Kal and Donnie crept through the house with no signs of life or activity in sight. They checked behind doors and in closets. Nothing. Place was abandoned. Gunfire and another large explosion outside rocked the house. The red and black rings of the giant sand worm slid past the kitchen windows followed by a death scream.

"Out the back," Kal ordered.

He paused when Donnie didn't respond. A glance and he realized why.

Donnie's face was suspended in a contorted look of pain and concern, his body frozen in place. He coughed and sputtered, grabbing at his throat suddenly unable to breathe. His gun dropped to the floor.

"Donnie? Man, what's—"

Kal knew without another word. Donnie coughed a small puff of red smoke into the air and dropped weakly to his knees. A hex. Kal held back the panic and sent his senses out into the house.

I know you're close, motherf—

Kal lunged just in time to dodge the black knife that split the wall over his head.

He aimed at the shadow moving in on him from across the kitchen. Fired. Hit only smoke.

In an instant another dagger was at his throat held by a figure in a trim black suit standing right behind him. Kal froze as Donnie continued to cough and choke.

"You should have quit while you were ahead," Bael whispered in a greasy voice behind his ear.

The point of the dagger pressed against Kal's windpipe and he watched Donnie cough up the red smoke, eyes rolling back into his head.

"You'd think I would learn," Kal muttered.

He paused a moment, baiting Bael to respond and as he started to speak, Kal rolled from his grip. A hard left to the knife forearm and a head butt in the nose later, Kal was at Donnie's side helping him shake off the effects of the conjurer's hex.

Bael came at him again with the knife and this time Kal grabbed the black blade from the wall. The men squared off. Donnie finished coughing and found his footing.

Bael licked his lips with a grin and lunged. Kal spun to the side, jabbed with his own blade and missed. They circled one another, eyes unblinking, feral.

"Where's Eden?" Kal demanded.

"Safe," Bael responded cryptically.

Kal lunged again and the ensuing scuffle resulted in bloody scratches for them both before they locked one another in a fierce grapple. Kal grumbled a defensive mantra that gave him a surge of strength he applied to overpowering the wiry-framed sorcerer, forcing him into the corner. Pushing with all his power and fury on the blade, Kal brought it to a rest right at Bael's throat.

"I'll send you straight to the Pit," Kal threatened, gritting his teeth and daring the pale skinny sorcerer to move.

Bael stared hard into Kal's eyes, deep into his soul. Psychic feedback erupted like uncontrolled static and showed the men little glimpses into his enemy's mind, hints at his deepest thoughts. Neither liked what he saw there. The deep mind of a shaman is not a pretty place.

"There's nothing you can do to stop this," Bael hissed. "*Mictlantecuhtli* will resurrect to destroy the diseased empire of man and cleanse the world for the next sun. The Pit is already coming for us all."

Kal froze. Fearful revelations sapped his strength as he contemplated Bael's words and the knife wavered. Bael grinned with glee as his words haunted the so-called Medicine Man.

Donnie aimed his gun over Kal's shoulder. "Didn't your calendar already run out?"

BAM! Fired a shot into the corner and hit only black smoke.

There was brief movement behind them and then the room was empty.

Kal's hearing erupted into a head-shredding ringing from the echo of the gunshot in his ear. He struggled to orient himself to his surroundings, stumbling and deaf.

"Find him!" he shouted.

The sound of sirens and helicopter blades arose outside and the scene of warfare and chaos turned to the commotion of full scale retreat as the gangs panicked. Donnie darted out the back door but Bael was nowhere in sight. The choppers were in the air however.

"Damnit, Kal, we have to go!"

Kal dropped the knife. "Mictlantecuhtli?"

"Come on!"

"But Eden..."

Kal paused to look for her in the hallway and the adjacent bedroom. No sign of Eden. His ears were still ringing so he didn't notice the black figure slipping from behind the door until Bael's grinning crocodile features were right in front of him. There was no time to react before the black dust in the man's hand was blown with one firm puff into Kal's face. He looked away but had already inhaled the first traces.

And that was plenty.

Cold winds buffeted his face and the world turned upside down. As the chemical surged through his bloodstream and into his brain, Kal was transported far away, dangling over an open pit ringed with teeth and a guttural growl like none he had ever heard came belching up from its acrid depths.

Kal's body collapsed in the hallway, his mind and soul pulled like gravity to the underworld, spinning in a ravaging twister of wind and smoke and debris.

He kept thinking of Eden and the dark ancient name that Bael had uttered.

Mictlantecuhtli...

He wasn't aware of Donnie coming back for him and scooping him up. He didn't notice the police lights and sirens around them as Donnie carried him on his shoulders across the desert dunes toward the place where the Jag was parked.

Donnie tried not to think about Kal's weight or the throbbing in his twisted ankle. The scene around him was chaos and he would be lucky to escape this one.

There were massive holes in the ground where the giant hell worm had thrashed around but it was long gone now that the Law Boys had arrived. The gangs tried to flee but several of them were nabbed or gunned down. A few Kranks and Hooligans managed to scramble out into the open desert but most fell behind. Darby's guys were nowhere to be found and Dre seemed to have made it out, one way or another.

"Put your weapons on the ground now!" came the megaphone voice from the chopper.

The Brujan soldiers refused to give up. They charged the Feds, guns blazing, forcing the cops to gun them down. Those that weren't shot, knelt to take their own lives on the point of a black blade.

Donnie made his way across the desert toward the Jag. Saw Gaines in the mix of badges and hurried that way to work his buddy for a favor. Gaines spotted him in the crowd and gave him a nod that parted him to the side and out of harm's way but Kal was too far gone to make sense of anything happening around him. His thoughts were jumbled and distant, his mind spinning in the dark twister.

Mictlantecuhtli...

2012 wasn't the fireworks extravaganza they had hoped for so they were doing it themselves.

They're trying to bring about the end of the fifth sun, this world age.

They want nothing less than Armageddon.

The confirmation of his fears and the dizzying, ravenous effects of the Oblivion dust coursing through him sent Kal's mind and soul into a tailspin that saw the world fall away, disappearing into a black hole before all went dark.

TWENTY-FIVE

KAL WAS STILL in the twister of hurricane winds and choking black smog, seemingly suspended upside down over some unfathomable abyss below.

Focus, Kal...

Concentrate...

He had seen firsthand the effects of Oblivion and the dark subterranean place it took its victims' souls. He couldn't let himself slip into that nest again. Wouldn't become another zombie victim of the Brujan devils. There was too much at stake. Something was happening out there. The world stood on the verge of a mass tear in the fabric of reality where the spirits of death and destruction would flow through in legions. Ancient evils were finding footholds in the world through this chemical dust and the will of twisted conjure men.

There was no Joos to save Kal this time and the demons swimming around in his gut would torture him until he finally lost himself to the unending Pit below.

And that's just what they did.

He had no choice amidst the churning vortex of the underworld but to fold himself up and let the spirit world take him. If he played his cards right, at least he could find someone down there with some answers.

Sounds faded. Light dwindled.

Kal drifted away from the world of form and life, into the murky shadows of the nether realm. Left his body behind so his soul could *deathwalk* across the In-Between like so many shamans of old.

He dropped out of his own mind and body, down below the world to a place just beneath the collective dream of reality. The feelings and weight of a solid form scattered into the ensuing grey smoky shadows and he came to rest in a place that continued to feel like hanging upside down.

The land of lost souls spread out around him.

This version of the world appeared a decaying husk as though some Armageddon had happened long ago. Amidst this endless grey waste, there were only vacant ghosts and wispy reminders of life. Bones and old stone.

A path wound through the shell of what must have once been downtown San Diego. Zombies shuffled mindlessly along the streets of busted asphalt, staring at their feet. Bodies hung from nooses overhead, swaying and turning slowly in the night fog that blanketed the landscape on all sides. The only sounds in the unhallowed hush were the creaking of the ropes and the distant clinking of bones.

This was the road through the underworld. And perhaps a glimmer of some possible future for the real world he had left behind.

Kal followed the road as it wound through the mist and shadows to a hilltop overlooking the charred husk of the city below.

Here the road ended at The Gate, that swirling vortex that draws all like a black hole to its inevitable omega point.

The psychedelic medicine man from Ocean Beach stood mesmerized by the swirling portal of ethereal light that twisted into nothingness between two black onyx sphinx statues standing guard over the mysterious doorway out of the universe.

"I've seen this..." Kal murmured to himself.

"In your dreams," answered a voice from the spinning portal.

Slowly and carefully, a form began to materialize in front of the Great Gate, a towering muscled figure with the head of a dog and eyes that burned like fire. Kal gulped down the nervous lump in his throat.

The Judge. The Jackal. Guardian of the Gate.

ANUBIS.

"You know I can't let you pass, Seeker," said the Gatekeeper and his voice cut through Kal's nerves like knives.

"I didn't come to ask for death," said Kal.

"Then why did you come?"

"I was hoping you could tell me," Kal answered as he stepped forward. His next words were interrupted by another bout of poisoned coughing. He clutched his chest, the pain and sickness still torturing him inside.

The howling of the demons he'd been battling and digesting created a distortion in the atmosphere around him, a white noise that was difficult to ignore. Anubis waved his bone scepter and blighted them like pests through the portal. The relief of having the sickness suddenly gone washed Kal to his knees and he caught his breath. Sweet relief.

"Ask away."

Kal was grateful for the reprieve from the swimming in his guts and took a moment to savor the freedom from his torment.

"Before I lose my patience," warned the Jackal.

"How is Mictlantecuhtli crossing worlds?" Kal asked, relieved to no longer be in agony, the torture instead replaced with a gaping empty hole like weightless drunkenness in the belly. He was feeling brave, even in the face of a god of judgment. "Things are already passing through. How do I stop it?"

"What makes you think he can be stopped?"

That wasn't what Kal was expecting.

"Because he must."

"You underestimate the dark gods," uttered Anubis in that nerve-grating tone.

"Then the world is doomed?" Kal scoffed. "That's not possible."

The Jackal stared blankly, a statue, an empty puppet.

Something wasn't right. Quite suddenly a feeling of abject dread passed through Kal, worse and more ominous than the hundred demons that had tortured him all the way to the Gate.

"Who are you?" he asked.

The Jackal's form gave a shudder as though it were nothing more than thin veil of fabric billowing in the deathly cold breeze of this foul place. The landscape stretched, distorted, and grew around them both as though Kal were shrinking and fading away. He stepped back and tried to maintain his balance even as the image of Anubis was swallowed by the dark space that wrapped and twisted around them. That space, a black hole, swallowed the Omega Gate and grew teeth the size of ship sails.

From that gaping maw rose a figure as black as the tar of the inner earth. Mictlantecuhtli's jagged bone teeth and clattering skeleton dominated the whole horizon and the Jackal headed judge was swallowed in his shadow.

"*BEEE HHOOLLLDDDDD!!*" bellowed a voice Kal perceived as a twist in his own brain matter, a gut-wrenching abomination of unholy sound.

Kal was a pale ghost and wondered if maybe this really was the end.

A massive step pyramid rose from the ground and towered over him. Standing atop its peak, posed like Kali with many arms of death, illuminated by the fires that flickered around her, was Eden. A dark, possessed version of Eden. The queen of the underworld blazed to life through Eden's form.

Kal stumbled back but the world was already wrapping around him, the vision consuming him, swallowing him whole. Like a dream gone out of control, the world contorted and a new scene grew up around him.

He stood amidst the crowd of an ancient Aztec mass, a hedonistic party and sacred ritual in the square beneath the pyramids. Revelers and music spun a cloud of confusion and wild expression as blood was spilled from sacrificial victims to flow like a river along the cobbled stones at their feet.

It was a Resurrection of ancient powers. A debt owed to them by our world.

A ceremony to end the age.

Flashes of a party in the desert hit Kal from the side and the dance brought a new vision to his mind, that of Athen's big moment, his big event, coinciding with...

The great reckoning of the Old American Gods.

That was it.

Oh God, that was it.

Res Fest. They were gathering at the festival to recreate this terrible black mass. Mictlan would use Eden as a gate and the revelers as fuel. The world would see one of the Old Ones born into the human dimension and all hell would literally break loose upon the world.

Kal struggled even as the pit was opening up beneath him. Even as the tentacles and vines were wrapping around him to pull him down into the darkness he had taunted for so long. He couldn't—he had to stop the Brujan plot.

"YOU TAUNT DEATH AND NOW DEATH HAS COME FOR YOU!" raged the unholy voice that twisted his mind into a painful knot.

Kal was out of ideas. He had come as far as he ever had into this mess that was the Otherworld. But now it had outmatched him.

He looked up into the eye of the black sun that shone overhead, waiting for his last damnation from the sky for his life of trickery, sorcery, drugs, and an arrogance that sought all the answers and secrets of the universe.

But what he saw wasn't a god. Certainly wasn't *the* God. It was a small shape in the middle of a black hole sun, flapping toward him on leathery wings. Red glowing eyes that swirled with his own spirit. A tiny winged imp that he thought he'd never see again.

Meklyn narrowed his wings and shot down out of the sky, right for Kal's outstretched fingers.

And then the ground swallowed him up.

And he was gone.

TWENTY-SIX

BRIGHT LIGHTS AND MUFFLED sounds drew him from his groggy state. Drool coated his chin and a lazy, drugged stare dressed up a bruised and swollen face.

Whatever had happened, it hurt.

"Hullo..."

The muscles in his face were sore and unresponsive but Kal was returning to consciousness. The room around him was a wash of bright, fluorescent light on sterile white walls. He tried to focus his blurry vision.

"Hullo?"

Felt like he had a ball of cotton in his mouth. He started to sit forward but found his arms restrained. Was this real? He was in a hospital ward somewhere after...

After what?

What had he been doing before?   He paused and listened to the white noise of the buzzing lights, fighting to dig up some valid memory of the last few days.

Nothing.

Strange visions of giant snakes and burning buildings. Gangs and gunfire and skull-faced sorcerers. Was that all a dream?

The door buzzed and opened, introducing a pair of stout men in white scrubs. Twins, by the looks of them or maybe Kal's vision was still a mess.

"Good morning, Kalvin," said the one on the left.

"How'd you sleep, huh?" echoed his twin on the right.

They started toward Kal and he recoiled against the chair. Through mumbling heavy lips he asked, "Where am I?"

"You're safe, Kalvin."

"In your own room."

Kal looked around. The room was a sterile hospital room of some sort with padding on the sharp corners and a tray of medicine cups on the sink. The orderlies smiled at him, a fake plastic kind of smile and Kal felt ill.

This wasn't happening. Couldn't be. He was in some kind of hospital, some psyche ward, some zoo. The handsome smiling twins unstrapped him, grabbed his arms, and hoisted him to his feet.

"Time for your morning checkup," said one.

"Stop it, I'm—What's happening?" Kal struggled, unknown drugs still immobilizing the majority of his muscles and half his brain activity.

"Don't you worry, Kalvin," said the other attendant. They took turns speaking. "Dr. Azmodi always fixes you up real nice."

Their passive, painted smiles did nothing to calm Kal's agitation. He tried to calm himself, remember his training, trying to relax. His heart rate was already high and the confusion was a tangible pain in his brain.

Last thing he remembered was the dream he was having about the snake and the witch doctors. But what came before? He didn't remember this hospital. Didn't remember his life.

Before he knew it, the attendants were lying him back on a bed and strapping his limbs in place once again. A bright light swiveled over his face and washed out his vision with painful bright light.

"Stop!" he yelled, voice still weak, but it was no use. They ignored him, going about their ultra-serious medical business.

"Donnie," Kal mumbled. "Where's Donnie?"

The men paused and looked at Kalvin.

"Get Donnie," he repeated.

They exchanged a wary glance and continued to set the room until the Doctor made his entrance. Kal heard the door and the footsteps but the bright light was blurring his vision. The smell of cheap cologne and hand sanitizer accompanied the looming presence of Dr. Azmodi and his voice was an oily, nasally thing.

"Ah, Mr. Renley, how are we feeling this morning?" he wheezed.

"Donnie..." Kal murmured. "Can't see. Move this light."

The bright light and its warmth were suddenly gone, replaced by the pale, boney face of the doctor, grey whiskers poking out from his sagging cheeks and yellow stains on his teeth. He leered at Kal with an uncomfortable fascination.

"Who's that you're calling for then?" he asked.

Kal cleared his head. This wasn't real, it couldn't be. Didn't make sense. He was caught in some kind of trance.

"Donnie," he repeated. "Eden. Where are they?"

The doctor shook his head in disappointment. "Tsk tsk, Kalvin. I thought we had made some progress."

Liar...

"What are you talking about? I want to see my friends!"

The doctor turned to his tray of tools. Sharp tools, electric tools, tools with teeth. A latex glove slapped over his hand.

"I must remind you once again that your name is Kalvin Renley. You suffered a severe drug overdose and a particularly violent suicide attempt."

He revved a drill, something that might be used to work on teeth. Kal was already resisting his words.

He's a liar, Kal, don't listen...

"There is no Donnie or Eden, these are figments you invented to deal with the trauma. Your mind is haunted by an imagination full of drugs and witchcraft."

The doctor stood over Kal with the drill.

"No..."

"You're apparently still quite ill, Kalvin," wheezed the boney doctor with the oversized ears and yellow teeth.

"No!"

Kal heard the drill. Heard the words echoing in his head. Was it true? Was he sick? Insane? All of this nonsense about magic and gods and drugs, was it a bunch of madness?

They call him the Medicine Man.

"They call me the Medicine Man," Kal mumbled as he squirmed away from the bright light and the drill and the "doctor" that smelled of old man breath. How did he get here?

How...?

"On the contrary, Mr. Renley," grinned Dr. Azmodi malevolently. "You're in a hospital for the deranged and disturbed. Your mother put you here after your suicide overdose. In here... *I'm* the medicine man."

The drill became a splatter of warm blood and a nuclear blast of pain across his skull as the tiny blade bored into Kal Renley's head.

The world convulsed and shuddered as he screamed and from somewhere overhead came the flapping wings of a familiar shape with glowing red eyes...

TWENTY-SEVEN

"WAKE UP."

The lingering nightmare sat like a fat hog on Kal's face and he found it difficult to move. Somewhere there was talking in a muffled, underwater quality. He half wondered if he was waking from another trip in his beach side shack. Or worse, maybe he was still in that horrible hospital.

"Wake up," called the voice again. "He's coming."

Kal forced his eyes open and let the blinding blur adjust to a somewhat normal range of vision. Meklyn was perched on his chest, coaxing him out of the underworld with his swirling eyes and Kal was never so glad to see him.

"Ah, Mek," he said groggily. "Where the hell are we?"

"Safe," was the reply he got but it wasn't Meklyn this time.

A blurry figure loomed over him and Kal sat bolt upright. He quickly wiped the substantial gunk from his eyes and shook off the grogginess. The room was dimly lit but familiar. The smell of the ocean greeted him pleasantly, followed by the piss mildew smell of his own ratty couch.

"How you doing?" Donnie asked.

"I don't know," answered Kal honestly. "Fine, I guess."

A quick glimpse of several small glass vials on the coffee table brought a familiar taste to his mouth and he knew Donnie had given him the Joos.

"Where'd you get it?"

Donnie sat down on the chair across from him. "Mab."

Shocker. Mab was the last person Kal expected to help him, let alone with Joos.

"How long was I out?"

"Three days."

"Three *days*?"

He glanced at Meklyn but the imp just shrugged and disappeared. Kal tried to piece together the visions he had, the underworld, the raid at the compound, Mictlan...

"Brought you back here after the raid. I wasn't sure what to do ut she—"

Kal had done the math in his head, best he could remember, and a sudden urgency gripped him.

"It's tonight!"

Donnie stopped his train of thought and looked at him.

"The Festival. The burn," Kal said, leaping to his feet in a panic. "The final ritual, Donnie, it's tonight!"

"What the hell are you talkin' about?"

Kal stood and caught his balance. "I need some air. Come on, I'll tell you in the car."

Donnie didn't ask any more questions. He'd had enough of waiting around anyway. Some answers would be nice right about now. He waited outside as Kal rummaged around for a few odds and ends in his shack and then led him down to the street.

Donnie's black and red jaguar was a sight to behold. A beast of the streets and Kal was glad to slip into her leather bucket seat and feel the wind on his face once again.

They drove through town and hopped on Highway 8 heading east out of the city.

Donnie caught Kal up to speed on the last three days.

After the fallout at the ranch, most of the Krank Street Krew were locked up or dead. That meant their neighbors, The Pistoleers, had an opening to move on their turf. Except the Krew had allies ready to stop that kind of action.

"Everyone's been acting way out of character," Donnie explained. "Been shoot outs and drive-bys in the Krank Street neighborhood for two days. Pockets of aggression breaking out all over the city. Whatever the Brujan cooked up out on that ranch, it's had ripple effects all over town."

Kal figured the confusion was understandable. Nobody knew what actually happened out there since few people would believe there was a giant snake eating people and a cadre of Mexican cartel soldiers practicing black magic. On Donnie's account, most think it was a drug trip that got out of hand and people ended up dead or arrested.

"What a mess," Kal muttered. The streets hadn't improved, he noted as they drove past a small group of zombie deadheads, shuffling mindlessly toward the desert.

"Funny you should mention Athen's festival," Donnie continued.

"Why's that?"

"He's been ramming this thing down everyone's throat. It's like he won't give up. He sent envoys to all the clans to encourage attendance, promising them their disputes will be settled in a final grudge match, winner takes all."

"He's insane."

"I was gonna go with fucked up and twisted," Donnie shrugged.

Kal thought for a minute. Athen was either completely oblivious to Xechan's plans for his big desert rave or he was in on the whole thing. That would explain his fervor for inviting the gangs. The more chaos and carnage at this thing, the better for the raising of Mictlan.

"That little shit."

Donnie nodded. "Shit got real."

"Anyone still loyal to us?" Kal asked.

"Your cure worked on Darby's girl so we've got him on a Wookie Life Debt till the end of his days," Donnie said with a smile. "Probably got the Primals if you want 'em."

"That'd get interesting."

"Couple of the north county beach clans. Enough to gather some guys but not to stand against what's happening at that festival."

"We don't have to stand against it, just disrupt it. Whole thing hinges on Eden and the big chief. We get to them, we end the madness and then it's just crowd control. It'll still be a mess but we just might prevent an all-out bloodbath and the possible coming of the Aztec apocalypse."

Donnie gave Kal a sideways glance and a grin spread across his face.

"Welcome back, buddy."

Kal smiled and the Jag roared down the highway toward an uncertain future.

TWENTY-EIGHT

IT HAD ALL COME down to this. Kal was supposed to be out of the game, living his life in secluded retirement after just a glimpse of the danger his gifts could bring to the world. But the gods had other plans for him. That girl had come into his life and asked for his help, had bewitched him in a way he didn't think was possible anymore, and he promised to help her. Now she was set to play a part in the awakening of an ancient Aztec death deity on the chain of a ruthless gang boss sorcerer.

These things happen.

To Kal Renley, anyway.

The drugs, the magic, the violence, it was all coming to a head in the middle of the desert and Kal had to be there to stop Armageddon before the party killed them all.

"There's a spot over there."

Kal and Donnie had jockeyed for hours on the east freeway along with hundreds of cars attempting to jam into the parking area off the main road. Cars were lined up for miles. The sun was just about to dip beneath the western horizon behind the line of traffic and the sky boiled with savage reds and oranges.

"This oughta be interesting," Donnie said as they passed a trio of naked, body-painted blondes with spiked collars.

"Don't get excited," Kal warned, eyes peeled for danger. "This thing is gonna turn on its head."

"Long as there's titties, it's a party."

The sun glared off the desert sand and Kal closed his eyes and stretched his subtle senses.

He could see them all. Bending his mind across horizons, Kal could see the clan bosses preparing for war. Darby kissing his daughter on the forehead and then nodding to his guys as they emerge from the warehouse with pieces of iron in hand. Dre standing proudly in front of what remained of his Krew with the look of vengeance on his face. Others too. The faces of generals and chiefs leading warriors into the fray. And then that dark cloud that cloaked el Brujan and their heathen warlord. The puppet master.

And Eden. If only he could see her face, a glimpse that she was okay, but the dark cloud obscured too.

The jag whipped into the last spot in a long row of VW vans and old cars.

"Ready?"

Kal opened his eyes to Donnie's expectant look.

"Let's go," Kal said and the boys stepped out of the Jag.

They made their way across the parched sand and through the crowd as the sun sank toward the ocean in the distance. The place had the typical trappings of a crowded music festival in the desert. Two stages across from one another with a massive crowd in the middle. A line of venders beneath tents and tarps. Port-o-Potties with long lines.

Then there were the more interesting features unique to the underground culture that Athen's events tended to attract. The punk rockers and heavy metal heads wandered in their respective tribes of wild hair and chain jewelry. The tribals and hippies were spinning fire and glow sticks. The suburban party kids rocked red Solo cups and backward ball caps doing belly shots and chest bumps. Little crowds formed around a steady beat to bust out dance-offs and rap battles. Place was a mish mash of the underground where anything goes, so long as it gets a rise out of someone.

Brujan soldiers were everywhere too. Kal could feel their energy on the wind and smell them like sickness. He just couldn't see them. Some of the security guards looked like they fit the bill but there was a lot going on. The eyes and ears of Xechan sifted through the crowd like spies in London square. Kal wondered if they were waiting for something.

...then he saw the zombie hoard.

Beyond the parked cars and roving cliques, they came like a wave. Walking for miles, they had been summoned to the desert and were now emerging from the fields and roads, mindlessly moving toward the source of warmth and music in the coming night. The soulless were descending on the ritual.

El Brujan had been cooking up Oblivion in their labs and the stuff had created legions of mindless walking zombies on the streets of San Diego and up the coast. These deadheads were now converging here.

And they weren't alone.

The gangs and clans were arriving too, each packing an arsenal prepared for war. The Gear Heads, the Krank Street Krew, South Side Locos, the Disfits and Hood Ratz. Vans and hummers and motorcycles rolled in from all directions. The Dirty Paws and Filthy Petes, a trio of the Diva Saints, even an envoy from the Pale Dragons as far north as San Francisco. As many as existed in the woven tapestry of underground punk drug culture along the coast, they were here for a Battle Royale. The prize was total control of the market, so Athen told them. Everything Donnie and Kal had done to bring about the truce was unraveling.

The red sun finally slipped beneath the horizon, signaling the witching hour, and the crowd roared and howled with delight.

That's when the mega-speakers crackled to life, calling everyone's attention to the stage with a loud, rolling thunder clap followed by a little electronic ditty. And then the voice of the man himself.

"Ladies and Gentlemen, Children of All Adult Ages!"

Spotlights swarmed the stage as colored beams shot heavenward, the whole venue coming to life with light and sound. The crowd hooted and howled like a barbarian hoard and a figure dressed in a trim white suit stepped to the front of the stage.

"Welcome to the concert event of your very lives," said Athen confidently and more than a little enthusiastic. The crowd broke into a roaring applause and the DJ dropped in a fat bass line that felt like the heartbeat of the world.

Dancing and leaping broke out in every direction around Donnie and Kal. The ritual was in play, the participants primed.

"Here we go," Kal said to the imp on his shoulder and Meklyn purred like a cat.

Movement swirled around the medicine man and the energies in the Earth began to pull at his feet as the chaos unfolded. He paid close attention to the mechanisms of the magic at hand, hoping to guess the direction of the swell that was gaining momentum.

The revelers partied, lost themselves in the dance and drums and drugs. Those who weren't zombies were offering up a vital life force to the atmosphere, a living excitement necessary for the energy of the spell. The zombie dead heads were something else, empty vessels whose souls were harvested like eggs on the other side, food for the newly reborn god.

Xechan's plan was to use the revelry for spell fuel, the party for trance. His dark God would consume the souls on the other side to fuel its emergence through the portal and then feast on the souls present at the rave.

And the portal was Eden.

Kal paused in the middle of the crowd. As far from the stage as he was, he could already sense Eden's presence. It was a small part of her, a tiny cry for help, but she was there, off at the edge of it all. He drifted into his trance and he could see them. The soldiers, the gangs, Bael slinking around behind the stage, and even the darkness that was Xechan.

"Whaddya got, buddy?" Donnie's voice broke into the trance.

"Push the violence out away from the middle as best you can," Kal said. "Damage control."

Donnie looked grimly at his friend. "Gonna get ugly either way."

"Be careful," Kal warned.

Donnie turned and led Darby and the other allies to a distraction point along the perimeter near the stage, unaware that Dre Daggers was wading through the crowd nearby.

Dre was looking for one group in particular. Took him a while to spot them but when he did, his whole Krew spread out to clear a space for him amidst the chaos. A vast open channel expanded between Dre and King Carlo of the Pistoleers.

"You fucked up, Carlo."

Carlo wiped the beer foam from his mustache and grabbed a massive serrated knife.

"I thought you'd never show," said Carlo.

Dre's lip twitched in rage and he pulled out a blade the size of his forearm.

Carlo smiled. "Let's dance."

Hoots and hollers erupted from the assembled crowd as the clan leaders circled one another. Vicious animal hunger in their eyes, they lunged and swiped.

Screams and scattering broke up one pocket of the crowd but the music and the magic had already gripped most of the minds. They were lost in the sound, the beat, the rhythm, the lights and colors and smell. Dancing and grinding and making out. Drinking and popping pills and smoking stashes. The ecstatic state was already a cloud over the arena and it was building toward a frenzy even as the gangs unleashed their hate and pride on one another.

BANG BANG went the gunshots but the crowd dismissed them as just another note in the soundtrack.

Donnie and the Gear Heads pushed the violence out away from the party as best they could but he nearly took a bullet himself. There were only so many things and people to hide behind and it was getting more out of control by the minute.

Kal had better hurry, was all Donnie could think to himself as he scanned the crowd for skull masks and clan faces.

KAL FOUND A PLACE to seclude himself, laying down in a prostrated position where he allowed his mind to dance down into a deep trance. He blocked out the gunfire and violence, the monkey screams and heathen screams, making it all part of the trance. Let himself fade downstream, traveling across the veil to the spirit side. He wasn't sure how he was going to do this but he had to save as many souls as he could.

BEHIND THE MAIN LIGHTS of the stage, amongst the pillars of iron that held the massive platform aloft, were the priests of el Brujan. Xechan had prepared the ritual space to suit his final victory. Burning censors of smoking compounds, little fires burning strange effigies, symbols smeared across every available surface.

His priests had done well. They already had several of the partiers in their thrall, pulling on their minds, compelling them to prostrate in worship to Xechan or strip naked as they danced to the sway of the electronic hypnosis.

Xechan watched, felt, and approved. Chaos was the queen of the night. He had prepared himself a long time for this. A thousand rituals and sacrifices to the dark gods and the Lord of Mictlan had forged him into something sinister and terrible. Now it was time to give the world its final farewell.

Shivering in a daze behind Xechan, cloaked in her own ceremonial black jaguar pelt, was his most precious piece of the equation.

"My Queen," he growled. "Are you ready?"

El Diablo took his lady by the hand and led her to the stage, presenting her to the world in all her horror.

Eden stood there looking out over the crowd, the vast expanse of space stretched out above their heads and a swaying crowd of worshippers at her feet. The desert was a multi-colored dream just on the other side of the veil that shielded her mind. She felt that energy deep inside her, it had been working its way into her core and it felt good. She felt the power of her true self, or so she thought. This was the expanded potential of her psychic energies. This was what Eden was meant to be.

She *was* the party. Every swaying body, every delirious mind, every flame and beat. She was the Goddess and the Queen. She was the earth itself and she was ready to erupt like a volcano.

Eden looked at Xechan, seeing both horror and glory, and nodded.

Something deep inside her was trying to resist but it wasn't nearly as powerful as the spirit yearning to come through to this world. They would give it the unholy birth it deserved, one way or another.

GUNFIRE PUNCTUATED THE dance and Donnie dodged a wayward fist. What started out as everyone's typical weekend music fest had evolved—or devolved—into the world's biggest mosh pit. Something—or someone—was getting into people's heads. He could see it.

The sound and lights created a dizzy miasma overhead, a color clash beneath the stars. Something eerie was creeping into the eyes of everyone present, regardless of what drugs they were on. Madness reigned. Bloodlust sent fists and knives flying, followed by the occasional spray of bullets.

"Darby!"

The Gear Headz weren't hard to pick out. The brutes stood a foot or more above everyone else. Darby nodded and waved Donnie over. Just as well. While Donnie swayed this way and that in the ocean of bodies, the Gear Headz were like pillars of stone that the water flowed around. Any ravers that got too close with their flying elbows and swinging fists, Ratchet close-lined them or put them out with a right hook.

"This is a Goddamn zoo!" Darby bellowed over the noise.

"This is just the beginning," Donnie warned. "We have to get to the stage."

Glad to have a clear goal, Darby nodded. He turned and waded into the crowd, his barrel chest parting the waters like a snow plow clearing Alaskan roads. Clobbered some punk with a Mohawk and literally picked a guy in a flannel shirt up by his neck and threw him over the outstretched hands of the mob.

Donnie fell in line behind the big beluga, gun in hand, dodging the oncoming fists.

THE MUSIC WAS a heartbeat that kept speeding up and, as it did, the intensity of the event ramped up with it. Fight or flight. The crowd was jumping now. Up and down. Up and down. Bouncing into one another.

Kal felt the vibrations of the music like an earthquake as he rolled free of his body and floated into the air in spirit. From up high it looked like a physics experiment. Bunch of particles locked together in a high-frequency vibration chamber, amped up and agitated, slamming into one another in a massive soup of chaos creating myriad combustible elements and fractured explosions. Place looked like a splatter of human emotion in multiple colors. From here he saw sound and felt color, the shape of the collective consciousness tactile as any shape on earth.

Keep an eye out, Mek.

His winged pet was flying circles overhead, senses transmitting extra data to Kal. Better than any guard dog he could have brought to the fight, Meklyn pointed out several hot spots, a potential threat from fire spinners nearby, and a location for the sick energy that was Xechan.

Kal scanned the stage. Brujan cultists were shuffling around the main stage but on the higher platform above the whole event stood

Eden. She was monstrously contorted, her spirit bloated with the foreign presence of the otherworld. Even so, it was Eden. Kal moved his spirit closer to the lights of the stage to get a better look, just over the DJ's head.

Eden had taken on the shape of a many-armed goddess, a hideous Kali Derva with wild hair and rows of fangs in place of her teeth. Her skin a pale blue, her eyes lost to an inky blackness. Something was opening up on this plane and she was the anchor. She swayed and danced to the rhythm, all but given over to the trance.

A deep, swaying, otherworldly trance.

Kal set his focus.

He could use that to cross over.

DJ IN-D-CENT WAS a ghost figure with giant headphones and sunglasses. His table deck glowed green and his hands worked the knobs and disks like an alien driving a ship. And that ship was a thousand bodies going mad.

As the crowd danced and thumped and cheered around the stage, the priests made their entrance. Music dropped to a reverberating pitch that wobbled the gravity of the place. Six hooded figures lined up along the stage and raised their hands to the night sky.

Laser lights shot heavenward and the rumble of the low bass shook the ground.

In unison their voices rocked the sound system.

"BELLOCH MICTLAN! *A O ma Rahn Mictlantecuhtli!*"

To anyone unfamiliar with occult ritual and ancient Aztec names of power, their chants and prayers may as well have been artsy vocals. The crowd responded in kind, repeating the mantra.

"BELLOCH MICTLAN! BELLOCH MICTLAN!"

Donnie and Darby watched from the foot of the stage as people raised their hands to the priests and offered up that vital life force. Some dropped down to prostrate and worship. Others stripped naked and gave themselves over to the hedonism.

"Come on!" Donnie urged.

Ratchet and Diggs climbed the stairs to one side of the platform, clobbering a bouncer with a boulder-sized fist that toppled him over the railing. As the music ramped back up to an ear-piercing, sphincter-thumping crescendo, Darby and the Gear Headz took the stage. Their act was one of knee-bashing with baseball bats and face-stomping cultists with heavy boots. Their act was violent and bloody and sent the priests scattering into defensive maneuvers but the crowd went wild for the carnage.

"Left!" called Diggs in time for Ratchet to duck the swipe of a black shiv.

He laughed at the puny weapon and grabbed the priest by his throat, lifting him off the ground.

"Thought this wouldn't be any fun!" he hollered to Darby and tossed the squirming priest into the crowd.

IT WAS HER FACE that drew him in, hidden beneath the façade of the goddess. Eden was trapped in the psychic barrier between worlds.   Kal aimed his consciousness at her and reached with his senses.

The party stretched away behind him into shifting smoke and distorted light.   The real Eden was in a grey void between worlds on her knees at the mouth of a long hallway that stretched into the spirit world behind her.

Reality bent, stretched, and she took shape as Kal got closer.

Soon as she saw him materializing before her, she burst into tears.

"I didn't know what to do, he's coming, I'm going to—"

"It's alright," Kal said, stepping forward. "I found you."

His form became more solid, even in this hallucinatory place. Enough to take her hand.

As they made contact, the world shuddered and a deep guttural wail screamed out of the tunnel.   Kal froze. He knew what it was. Or, rather, *who*.

There were clinking bones with every movement and a powerful thud with every step.

The Bone Lord gave a loud screech of triumph as a rotting hand scooped up a handful of red fish eggs, the spirit shells of human souls, and shoveled them into his fanged mouth.

Mictlantecuhtli, God of Death and Pestilence, took another step toward the world.

"We have to go," Kal said and turned toward the party.

But Xechan was already there.

A looming specter of himself, projected across the veil, Xechan was fearsome and striking.

He dropped the royal jaguar fur from his shoulders revealing his chiseled, inked fortress of devotion. Dark energy gathered at his eyes and reality bent around him.

"You dare intervene in another shaman's rite."

Kal set his jaw. "When I'm in the mood."

They squared off a moment, sizing one another up. Two men who have crossed the veil, conjured spirits, and spoken to gods have little to say to one another and they both knew it. There was only one thing left to do.

And Kal was ready for a fight.

MEANWHILE, XECHAN'S BODY rested in a circle drawn on the platform behind Eden. Eden's body, possessed by the awakening Queen of Chaos, stood above the crowd, dancing and swaying with many arms and fangs and a long whipping tongue. A beastly version of herself.

The jumbotrons all projected her image over the crowd larger than life. Like a goddess, Eden-turned-Kali-Chaos gleamed against the starry night sky and blessed the revelry as the party raged on.

"This is the greatest show I've ever seen!" shouted a guy near the stage, face covered in glowing paint.

Nearby a trio of shambling zombies had their souls consumed by a death god and dropped to the dirt, inert corpses on the field.

"Rock and Roll!" someone shouted.

DONNIE ENJOYED LAYING a beating on the Brujan cultists, thinking of Miles with every blow. And though he may not admit it openly, when the hooded idiot with the pierced lips came charging at him with a wicked knife, his gun made no hesitation to raise and fire two rounds into the lunatic's head, giving him a sick satisfaction.

The priests dispatched to the amusement of the crowd, Donnie took note of the Brujan soldiers filtering through the masses toward the stage. Gunshots fired his direction, ripping down lights and clanging off metal as the crowd cheered.

Donnie ducked out of the way and saw Diggs on the ground looking shriveled up like a piece of fruit dried in the sun. A Brujan priest looked up from his wicked work and Donnie grew sick with rage. His gun wasn't fast enough though. Seeing the curse that took one of his loyal friends, Darby came raging across the stage, giant wrench in hand, and smashed the cultist's face like a wet sponge. Blood pooled on the stage.

High above them on the platform, Eden-turned-Lady-Chaos screamed a high shrill squeal into the night sky. The music changed. The place got darker.

"Next phase," shouted Donnie. "Hurry!"

MINDS COLLIDED, RIPPED, shredded, and strained on the Astral Plane.

Kal grunted and growled as he exerted as much mental willpower as he could muster. A clash of minds on the spirit plane was like each shaman shoving his fingers in the other's eye sockets and pushing. His brain hurt deeply and nearly hemorrhaged from the stress.

Colors and lights and pain went electric all around him and all Kal could do was gather up the piss and vinegar in his veins to force his own electric spirit at Xechan's mind with the ferocity of a cornered tiger.

El Diablo countered with a vicious swipe of his clawed hands and the ensuing psychic tug of war sent both shamans spiraling in circles around one another, two forces colliding.

Kal ducked and pushed through a hole in Xechan's defense a second time. Their spectral bodies collided in an explosion of sparks and they wrestled like demons in the ether. Eden shrieked and covered her eyes, shielded her mind. The explosion was point blank and the fallout was white hot fire.

"Kal!"

But he was locked in a grapple. Spinning, tumbling, twisting…

Xechan transmitted taunting images to Kal, tried to make him small and ridiculous. That's how these things worked, he was forcing his raw personality on Kal and, considering the guy was convinced of his own divinity, it was formidable.

Kal was under no illusions of personal grandiosity but he was confident in two things; that he had been through a lot of hell and he was a tough motherfucker.

Kal pummeled Xechan with fists the size of boulders, swelling up with magnetic fiery energy and the blows left singed black swathes across the sorcerer's tattooed form.

Xechan grew frustrated and pushed away.

Both shamans calmed their breath and stilled their minds, circling one another on the astral like opposing electrons in limited space.

"You have no idea what you're a part of," Xechan grunted.

"I know enough."

"The world must be cleansed."

"The world's always been dirty, man. You don't get to clean it up with more blood," Kal grumbled.

The Brujo growled and launched another volley of every barbed and aggressive thought and vibration in his being right at Kal's consciousness as he surged forward to hammer the medicine man to his knees.

Eden was pulled between worlds and the overwhelming surge of chaos that was bringing something through that long, cold tunnel sapped her of her power and energy.

She found only the desperate plea of "No no no no no please, this can't be happening . . ."

She hoped and she prayed and the energy poured out of her, Kal could feel it.

And he could use it.

MEKLYN CIRCLED OVERHEAD, keeping a close watch on the chord between Kal and his body. A few drunkards stumbled close to Kal's hiding place. Meklyn swooped down to land on a tall speaker as they laughed and prodded at Kal's unconscious form.

"Dude is so passed out!" one chuckled.

Meklyn drew a deep breath and belched a spray of flames that startled the curious drunks and sent them tearing off in the opposite direction.

Come on, Kal.

THE NOISE AND THE beat skipped and jumped as Donnie climbed the ladder that led to the upper platform. The Gear Headz braced themselves for the onslaught of Brujan soldiers that swarmed the side steps, firing a spray of bullets in their direction.

Darby and his guys ducked behind the steel pillars of the stage and sprang out to meet the soldiers hand to hand, grabbing their guns and knocking them aside. As expected, the skull-faced ninjas weren't so hot without their machine guns.

Seeing Diggs with that hideous curse laid out on the stage sent Darby and Ratchet into a frenzy along with their other clansmen. The group turned into raging barbarians, ripping and goring into the masked soldiers.

Donnie heard the death screams as he neared the upper platform.

THE RATTLING BONES of Mictlan clambered along the tunnel as the ancient God made the soul eggs his feast. His wail, as unearthly as any sound, warped and bent the reality around the wrestling witch doctors, shaking them loose from one another.

Kal rolled to the side and squared himself with Xechan. The brujo leaped and the brain-wrenching psychic battle continued. Kal was putting up a good fight but he may as well have been wrestling a lion. His strength was fading fast.

Eden closed her eyes and fought the Goddess energy that had overtaken her frontal thoughts. She focused on her concern for Kal even as the tall, boney Mictlan lumbered up the tunnel close enough to reach out for them both.

She knew how it worked, she had to concentrate her thoughts. Ball them up like a weapon. Her mind was reeling but she focused everything she had on Xechan. Every ounce of fear and adrenaline coursing through her, she pulled all of it together and, one silent prayer to the Gods, sent a blast wave of pure thought energy—all her anger and pain, all that repressed terror and self-loathing, all of it that landed her in the gutter and at the feet of *el diablo*—it all went roaring across the spirit plane to kick Xechan square in the chest.

He stumbled back just enough to give Kal an opening. One last focused blast sent Xechan spinning across the murky threshold and into the tunnel where his god was waiting. In the tunnel, his form turned to smoke and ash, a faded glimmer like a dying memory.

"No..." Xechan muttered, looking down at himself in horror.

Mictlan reached out for him, a massive corpse-like hand putrid with the stench of decay.

"Abort!" Xechan called in hopes that his priests would hear his call.

"It's no use," Kal said, solemn and still. "There's no way to go back."

The truth hit Xechan like a shotgun blast to the chest. He groped with his thoughts, willing it to be false, but Kal was right.

On the other side, standing on the platform over Xechan's bleeding body, gun still smoking, was Donnie. Cultists in black robes lay across the stage. Darby's bat covered in blood, his barrel chest heaving from the battle frenzy.

The Goddess Eden with her many dancing arms fell to her knees, her image flickering like a hologram. The arms faded. The demonic façade dissolved. There was just Eden.

Over the veil, Eden's psychic projection stepped close to Kal, gripped him tight, and they watched through the translucent wall as Mictlantecuhtli squeezed Xechan's soul and shoved him in that toothy maw, ripping the zealot to pieces and devouring him whole as the sorcerer's screams tore across all worlds.

Kal pulled Eden close.

"Now, Meklyn!"

The imp leaped onto Kal's chest with the force of a colorful explosion and in a snap, Kal awoke into the world of flesh, the party raging around him.

On stage, Eden woke with groggy eyes and looked out at the night to see the crowd roaring below her in a frenzied mosh pit. Donnie's hand appeared to help her stand and she took it, dizzy at first but managing to find her footing.

"You okay?" Donnie asked her.

Eden nodded and he helped her down the ladder to the stage. Her head swimming, she saw Athen emerge from the side stairs and stalk across the stage.

"Donnie, what the hell are you doing?!"

Donnie turned and held his gun to Athen's face. The weasel put his hands up and took a step back.

"Whoa, whoa, easy brother."

"Don't *brother* me, Athen. You led the clans to a slaughter. You did all of this!"

Donnie cocked the hammer back on his gun and Athen's world slipped away from him. He saw Xechan and the cult of el Brujan dead on the floor. Saw Eden staring daggers at him.

"Donnie, come on. You know as well as I do that the market is better for everyone if the gangs are at each other's throats."

"Better for you."

"Donnie, man, come on."

Out across the festival grounds, in the crowd where the frenzy of the spell was dying down and the music had changed abruptly, stood the clans.

Dre looked at King Carlo and Hoolio. Each felt as though he had awakened from a dream.

Some kind of sleepwalking slumber. Some enchantment.

They glanced around at one another. At the carnage. The mess.

Above them on the jumbotrons that gleamed against the night sky was Athen's face at the end of Donnie's gun. They heard his voice. His confession.

"Donnie come on, we can run this town together. Hell, we could rule the whole coast!"

"No, Athen. No more ruling for you. Your reign has ended."

Kal joined his friends at the back of the stage as Athen continued to plead for mercy.

It was no use.

Dre, Darby, Hoolio, and King Carlo followed Kal up the steps, venom in their eyes.

"We'll take it from here," said Dre.

Athen shrugged and opened his arms to receive his judgment like some arrogant martyr. Donnie wasn't waiting. He fired two quick shots through his head to end it all right then and there.

Athen just looked at him with the smirk they had all grown to loathe. His form flickered and faded away, a hologram blipping out of existence.

The music stopped.

The screens went blank.

The lights died.

The grand desert ritual they had called Res Fest was done and its Master of Ceremonies was gone.

TWENTY-NINE

DONNE, KAL, AND EDEN made it to the Jag, surrounded by other cars and vans. Eden leaned against the vehicle, clutching her stomach which still swarmed with a sick, wormy feeling.

"You okay?" Kal asked.

"I will be," she said. "I think."

He pulled her shirt down in the back to have a look at the tattoo. It was still there but the writhing evil that had previously animated it seemed to have gone. It didn't respond to his touch either.

"This house is clear," he said with a grin and Eden smiled. First real smile he'd seen from her yet.

"I don't know about you two but I could use a strong drink," Donnie said, slipping into the driver's seat.

Kal and Eden climbed in.

"I'm thinking Margaritas in Baja."

"Please not Mexico. Not yet," Donnie muttered as the car fired up and he put it in drive.

"How about Canada?" Kal said, leaning his head back to feel the cool wind whip against his face.

"How about my fucking condo and we'll go from there," said Donnie.

Eden and Kal were content despite it all.

"Deal."

THIRTY

THE ELEVATOR WAS SLEEK stainless steel with a plush maroon carpet and opened with a ding to the thirty third floor of the Omni hotel. A pair of polished black shoes stepped out and padded calmly down the hall. They belonged to a man in trim black suit, black tie, and rosy red sunglasses.

Bael knocked on the door of an expensive suite.

The door opened and he was greeted by a grey-haired Englishman in a formal tuxedo. The man nodded and showed Bael into the royal suite, surrounded by deep magenta drapes and solid gold trim.

"Frater Bael," said a voice.

"Frater Condor," Bael replied.

The brother they called Condor sat relaxed on a black suede couch with a number of other finely dressed gentlemen wreathed in clouds of smoke around the parlor. As Bael, who now seemed the more common of the group, stepped near and waited patiently, Condor reached out a gloved hand to shake.

"You have done well."

Bael gave the customary grip and nodded graciously.

"The entity did not cross over," said Bael, who had been expecting a reprimand.

"Nonetheless, it was a successful experiment," Condor mused.

"I'm glad the Order is pleased," said Bael, hiding his confusion.

Condor passed a hand over his greasy hair and a twinkle in his cat-like eyes caught the light. He adjusted his tie and asked, "Are you ready for your next assignment?"

Bael suppressed the twitch of a smile in the corner of his mouth.

"Very."

"Gentlemen, get this man a brandy."

ACKNOWLEDGEMENTS

Every book is the product of more than one person and I owe a great debt of gratitude to several rather amazing human creatures.

First, a very special thanks to my wife and partner-in-crime, Cynthia, for putting up with my spaced-out shenanigans and telling me over and over again that I can do this. Thank you for making this dream possible.

My thanks to Jason Corron for a kickass cover design and the first fully realized Medicine Man artwork.

A big thanks to an exceptional network of fellow creatives and beta readers who have been kind enough to review my work and, on occasion, tear it to smithereens; Timothy W. Boyd, Nathan Rupp, Rachel Riggs, Ellie Noel, the Archmage Keith Kelly, and Mr. Joe Cincotti. Countless others are out there and my gratitude goes to you as well.

Many thank you's to my awesome parents, brother, and extended family for offering pure encouragement, even when I doubted myself.

And, finally, to all the misfits and fringe-dwellers I've met on the road and across the interwebs as we wind our way through the apocalypse; Keep reading so I can keep writing!

ABOUT THE AUTHOR

Joshua Ryan Ogg has worked in entertainment media and digital marketing for close to a decade. Oblivion is his first published novel. He can usually be found in Ohio or California with his wife and two children.

Josh loves to connect with readers on social media and maintains a blog full of half-drunken ramblings and utter nonsense at

www.joshuaryanogg.com

ISBN-13: 978-0-692-38452-7